MEDOCINO MENACE

BETH HOWES

ReGeJe Press
Sacramento, California

Mendocino Menace, Copyright © 1998 by Elizabeth Howes

For information, address ReGeJe press, PO Box 293442 Sacramento CA 95829

ISBN 0-9639147-0-7

cover art, ©   Ibandan Baluba
cover design   J. Banks
               Raul Echauri

First Edition November 1998

10 9 8 7 6 5 4 3 2 1

I wish to thank those dear friends and relatives who pushed me into writing many years ago and especially those close to me who continued to believe in MENDOCINO MENACE and other pieces of my writing.

My deceased Mother, Vivian, and her sister, Edna, encouraged me as a child to put my ideas on paper.

Later, my teacher and friend, Lou Foley, reawakened this interest. One friend, Dorothea Gould, now deceased, listened to every one of my tales and made suggestions.

Others who had faith in me and made MENDOCINO MENACE possible were my sister, Claire Dennis, and Penny Warner.

Most of all I thank my wonderful husband, Ed, who endured burned and cold dinners when I neglected the kitchen while preparing another murder scene or delving into a reference work.

Beth Howes

CHAPTER ONE

I could hear the sea lions barking on the fog-covered rocks a few yards offshore as I threaded my way down the slippery path to the cove below our cabin. Some of the man-made risers on the trail down the steep descent were worn and splintered and offered little support for my feet, but I trusted to luck and let go of my last firm handhold on a trail side shrub, as I gingerly continued down to the narrow rocky beach. The tide was out, and a few small sea creatures wriggled in the remaining shallow pools.

I inched my way across the exposed rocks, slipping once and skinning a knee in the process. Squatting beside one of the tide pools, I touched a sea anemone that opened its mouth in its attempt to swallow my finger. Smarting from this encounter with the creature's sting, I trailed my hand in the salty water of another pool to search for a sand dollar to add to my collection.

This small, isolated cove had been my refuge these past five years. My husband Ted and I had decided to move from our home in the Central Valley to this part of the Mendocino County coast, located about a hundred miles north of San Francisco, after his retirement. During his thirty years as a history professor at the university we had enjoyed many pleasant vacations with our family on this part of the coast. Soon after we began seriously looking for our new home, we found this house which seemed to be just what we wanted. While Ted checked the plumbing and wiring with a couple of professionals and dickered with the real estate agent, I wandered down to the water's edge; looked out on the lonely stretch of sea and vowed this place would be our home.

This morning while I played in the tide pool, I lost track of time. The only sound, besides an occasional sea lion bark, was the lapping of the water against the large rocks. A glance at my watch as I got up to stretch my legs, reminded me of the youngsters up in the cabin. I was brushing the sand off my jeans and hands, when I heard voices. Was Ted coming down to look for me? No. These were strangers' voices coming over the water.

There was no place to land a boat here. Only a raft could skim over the rocky shoreline. Perhaps the people aboard were searching for the next cove, where fishing boats often moored. The voices were getting closer. Then, through the thinning fog I saw them, two men in wetsuits. They were so busy guiding their rubber raft toward shore that they had not spotted me.

"Watch it, dummy," the older, stockier man growled as the raft scraped against a half-submerged rock.

His partner jumped into the shallow water and pushed the raft past the rock. It was then that both men saw me.

Heaving his bulk out of the raft, the older man muttered, "What the hell's a snoopy woman doing down here?"

Irritated by the words I wasn't supposed to hear, I said, "Watching for trespassers trying to sneak onto my property." When the younger man pulled the raft toward another hidden hazard, I added, "Careful, young fellow. That rock could rip your craft in two."

When the danger was over, the older man splashed his way through the swirling surf toward me. A smile played across his face as he offered me his gnarled hand. "Aren't you going to welcome your trespassers?"

"I might as well, but why did you make for this cove? The one north of here is lots easier to reach" Before he could answer, I added, "Don't tell me you were looking for abalone. There haven't been any around here for years."

"Which do you want me to answer first—why we beached here, or whether we're searching for abalone?"

"It makes no difference. You'll choose the story you like best."

"Salty, aren't you?"

"Just as salty and wet as you," I replied, watching the second man lift the raft onto his broad shoulders and flap his flipper-clad feet toward us.

"No sense standing here waiting for the tide to cut us off from the beach," the older man said, offering me his arm. "Come on, I'll help you up those rickety steps over there."

"I can totter over to them by myself," I said, turning inland and beginning the hazardous walk over the wet rocks.

While I labored up the path, the older man introduced himself. "I'm Joe Gilliam, and my friend here is Kent O'Brien. And you?"

Ignoring his question I looked back at Kent O'Brien struggling to keep his balance on the slippery rocks. "Let Mr. Gilliam give you a hand with that raft. You'll need a free hand to crawl part of the way up the side of the cliff."

"Snoopy and bossy!" Joe Gilliam said, reaching back and hoisting one edge of the raft onto his shoulder.

As the two of them struggled up the cliff steps, Joe Gilliam said, "You live in that house on the point?"

Gasping for breath, I stopped at a shelf along the path and said, "Yes, that's our place. Sorry I didn't introduce myself. I'm Kay Roberts, the snoopy woman who plays in tide pools while watching for trespassers. Where are you two from?"

"We're renting a place down the road. The Allison house. Rustic but comfortable. Do you know it?"

"Everybody around here knows that place. Caught any rats yet?"

"No, but we'll keep trying. Especially since you say we can't bag any abalone off these rocks. Might as well try a rat stew."

"Add a little onion to bring out the flavor," I said, laughing at Joe.

By now we'd reached the first sturdy bushes which bordered the rough-hewn steps. I grabbed the shrub branches to

7

help me make it up the next steep step. Soon we were on top of the knoll overlooking the sea and taking the easy walk the last few yards to our cabin. Ted stood in the doorway waiting for me. "Breakfast's almost ready. Did you bring anything for me to throw into the pot?" Ted asked.

"Not to throw into the pot, but to introduce to you. They came right out of the sea toward me while I was playing in a tide pool. They're headed for the Allison place." Turning to the two men, I said, "Joe and Kent, this is my husband, Ted. He prefers sleep to a crawl down to the beach first thing in the morning"

"Glad to meet you. Care for a cup of coffee before you walk on over to your house?"

Before the men could answer, two youngsters bounded out the door and almost knocked me over with their enthusiastic greeting. "Grandma, we thought you'd never get back so we could eat. Catch anything?"

"Yes, these two gentlemen?" I introduced six-year-old Will and four-year-old Tom to the rafters.

"Go on with your breakfast?"Joe said. "But we will take you up on that cup of coffee."

While we ate, the strangers asked us about the area. Were most people here summer visitors? Was there much building going on here?

When we asked them how long they planned to stay, they were vague. Maybe a week, maybe as long as a month. It depended on whether they could find a good spot to study the sea lions nearby.

"Marine biologists?" Ted asked.

The two men looked at one another before Joe said, "Not professionals. Just a couple of amateurs" Getting up and starting for the door, he added, "We'd better head back to the house to look for those rats, ma'am. Thanks for the coffee."

"Don't forget the onion?"I called after them.

"What are you talking about? Rats? Onion?" Ted asked, as Will and Tom trailed Joe and Kent up the driveway.

When I told Ted about my experience down on the beach,

he said, "They may have paddled over from the sea lions' rookery to the north of us" Getting up and scratching his unshaven face, he added, "Any sensible seaman would have gone into that cove by the rookery. It's easier docking and closer to the Allison place. Are you sure there wasn't a fishing boat anchored off shore?"

"How could I tell in that fog? They were almost to shore when I heard their voices, and I didn't see them until they were into the shallow water" A chill went through me. "Maybe they had planned to come into our cove. But why?" I asked Ted.

Glancing at the empty plates of the boys. I remembered their stalking after the men. They should be back here by now . "I'd better check on the youngsters." When Ted announced he was going into town.to the post office, I linked my arm through his and walked with him to the highway to begin his two mile jaunt and to start my looking for our grandsons.

"If you see Will and Tom, send them back?" I said to Ted as I left him and headed in the direction of the Allison house. I spotted the boys tailing the men and ducking into the ditch beside the road whenever either man glanced over his shoulder. "They will tire of this game and return to the house soon?"I muttered to myself and began enjoying the cool of the morning.

While I ambled along the road, I stopped occasionally to pluck a berry and pop it into my mouth. So sweet and juicy. Between berry picking and dodging the on-coming cars, I began to plan for the arrival of the boys' parents that afternoon. Our son, Lewis, and daughter-in-law, Lora, were driving up from the valley. "I hope she's not car sick this time?"I said to myself remembering her trip up here last month to bring the boys. "This twisting road is enough to give the heaves to anyone, let alone a pregnant woman."

The morning fog had dissipated. The ocean sparkled in brilliant sunshine. Off on the horizon I could see the dark outline of a ship, probably a tanker. Closer to land there were several fishing boats. Had one of them dropped our morning visitors and their raft into the waters near our cove?

Before I could think more about the two men, I saw Will and Tom racing along the road toward me. I braced myself and held out my arms to catch these flying "unguided missiles," hoping I wouldn't be bowled over with their momentum.

"Grandma?" Tom said. "Those guys have a big panel truck in the driveway."

"And it's got one of those radar scanners on its roof?"Will added. "They went right to their truck instead of going into the house. While we watched, an antenna rose out of the truck."

"They are just a lot fancier than we are, boys. Maybe they were telling their sons about their morning rafting." I felt the boys weren't buying my story. Trying to sound unconcerned, I added, "Let's go back to the house to get a couple of pails for berry picking. Want pie with vanilla ice cream for supper?"

"Sure do?"they said and took off down the road.

"Beat you to the cabin, Will?" Tom shouted, churning his short legs as he ran ahead of his brother.

They were already coming out of the cabin with pails when I turned into our yard. "Coming, Grandma?" they asked.

"No. You choose the best berries, and I'll have the pie crust ready when you return." As the boys turned back and waved to me, I yelled, "Don't let the bramble bushes stick you. They don't like to give up their berries."

Ted was coming down the road from town as I started back toward the house. He had his hands full, sorting through the mail he'd picked up at the post office. I spotted the daily newspaper tucked under his arm.

"Letter from our son Eddie. Want me to read it to you?"

"Sure, while I roll out pie crust" I caught a glimpse of the headline, when Ted dropped the paper on the table. "Moon rocks, sea water! Have our scientists gone crazy?"

"Take it easy, Kay. Must be the sun's effecting you"

"Don't be ridiculous. Look at that lead story."

Handing the mail to me, Ted spread out the front page and read, "Moonrocks, sea water --future energy source "Well I'll be darned. And it goes on to say, Japanese scientist pushes helium-3 fusion'. Wait until we show this to Lewis and Lora!"

"See, I didn't have a sun stroke?"I said, snatching the paper from him. "Energy from moon rocks. How do they get them to Earth?"

"I guess we'd better read the article and find out about those rocks." While Ted sank down in his favorite leather chair and fumbled around for his glasses, he added, "Those two men don't look like vacationers to me. Did you see their eyes casing our place? They were friendly enough, but they're not what they seem"

I felt a pang of misgiving at his words. Ted, like me, felt there was more to these strangers than they were admitting. Of course, we had just met them. What did we expect, their life stories?

CHAPTER TWO

I dangled Ted's glasses in front of him and said, "Let's do our chores before we read Eddie's letter and the paper."

Groaning, Ted creaked out of the chair and headed for the linen closet. "No rest for the wicked," he mumbled before disappearing with an armful of sheets and pillow cases into the bedroom.

While he made the bed for Lora and Lewis, I rolled out the pie dough and started a chicken in the slow cooker. When we finished our tasks, Ted pulled out Eddie's letter. He read, "Ready for a visit from your traveling son? The boss finally realized what a gem he has in me and has given me a great assignment—to study and photograph the coast in your area. My trusty camera and I'll arrive next Thursday. First night supper's on me. Love, E."

"As modest as ever, our Eddie," Ted said, getting up and putting the letter on the desk. "It will be good to have him with us." He picked up the newspaper. "Come outside, Kay. You can sit in the rocker, while I read to you about that new moon rock source of energy."

"No chair for me. I'll jump on my trampoline, while you read."

Unfolding the newspaper, Ted began the item. "A Japanese scientist believes moon rocks hold all the energy the world will need for centuries."

"Great, but how do we get them to Earth?"

"Patience, Kay, and listen. This scientist thinks that within ten to twenty years, fusion reactors using helium-3 extracted from the rocks and hydrogen from sea water could provide energy that is cheap, efficient and not radioactive. And get this. Moon rocks ferried to Earth could provide enough helium-3 to last four hundred years, he thinks; and there is still more of this resource on Mars and Jupiter."

While I jogged in place, I began to envision men and women, encased in space suits, picking away at rocks on the moon and loading them into a waiting space ship to ferry helium-3 rich rocks to Earth. The cargo doors would close, and the ship would blast off for Earth. I could see them zooming down in a remote part of the world edging a body of salt water. Close by I spotted in my imagination their destination, a reactor ready to join this raw material with hydrogen from the sea to produce instant energy.

I stopped my jumping long enough to look out at the now glassy ocean. Could this be the spot where the three nations, the United States, Japan and Russia, might build such a reactor? Perhaps the project would be spread among the three nations. I shuddered, thinking about tearing up our coastline for such an undertaking.

I was jarred back to reality by Will's and Tom's stomping up the steps and Tom's yelling, "Hey, Grandma, look at all the berries we picked for you. While Will chimed in with "Got the pie dough ready?" Tom lifted his berry-stained face for me to kiss.

"Sure," I said, stopping my exercise and putting the trampoline in the closet. "Come out to the sink and help me wash the berries. Mmm, good," I added dropping a large juicy one in my mouth. Tousling Tom's silky hair, I asked, "Are you guys hungry, or did you fill up on berries?"

"Yeah, I'm starved, Grandma," Will said. "Can we have peanut butter sandwiches and milk shakes?"

"Sandwiches and milk shakes coming right up. You know where I keep the chocolate."

Filled with lunch, the boys settled down with their picture

13

books and soon fell asleep. The aroma of the freshly baked pies wafted through the house as I sat at the kitchen table working on a crossword puzzle.

By late afternoon dark clouds were moving in close to shore, and the ocean had turned an ominous gray-green. The first drops of rain splashed on the porch steps as Lew and Lora pulled into the driveway. The four of us rushed out to greet them. I carried an open umbrella to shield Lora from the elements while Ted held another one over Lew, who unloaded the trunk of his car.

Lora was shaking when I put my free arm around her and led her into the house.

"Twisting road get to you?" I asked.

"That and a pileup a few miles south of here. What a mess!"

"How awful! How many cars were involved?" Studying her face, I asked, "Are you and Lew all right?"

"We were lucky. Five more minutes and we might be among the statistics. A pickup truck smashed into a panel truck, but other cars skidded into the wreck and added to the havoc. The highway patrol hadn't arrived when we drove up to the scene, but some man had the good sense to get out and direct traffic around the line of fender benders and the two trucks."

As she mounted the steps, Lora continued. "We heard sirens screaming down the road from the north and saw the first highway patrol cars arrive. While we waited to pass, we saw an ambulance brake to a stop in front of the panel truck. When it was our turn to inch around the scene, we saw the ambulance attendants lift a man out of the panel truck."

Lora stopped talking and held out her arms to Will and Tom. Both tried to climb into her lap. "Not enough room," she said, pointing to her swelling abdomen before hugging the boys. "Your little brother is taking up all the space."

"Is he asleep?" Tom asked. "Must be. I don't hear him," he said, putting his ear to his mother's belly.

There was no more talk of the highway accident until after supper when Ted turned on the TV to get the local news.

"One of the two men in that panel truck died a few minutes

ago," the announcer said. "The driver of the pickup which rammed into the panel truck and spun out of control is still missing. Witnesses saw him jump from the smoking truck and run into the woods."

"That's the accident we saw," Lora cried, pointing to the screen.

"Shh. They're telling more about it," Lew said, leaning toward the TV.

Another picture of the overturned panel truck flashed across the screen.

"It's just like the one those men staying at the Allison house have," Will said, crawling closer to the TV.

"There are probably hundreds like it driving up and down the road every day," his dad said. "Who's staying at the Allison house? It's been empty for years."

"A couple of men, Joe Gilliam and Kent O'Brien," I said and told Lew and Lora about my encounter with them. Turning to the boys, I added, "We'll walk up there tomorrow when the rain lets up and see whether their van is still in the driveway."

"That won't tell you anything. They could be out sketching those sea lions they talked about," Ted reminded me.

The commercials were over, and the announcer came back on TV saying, "There's been a break in that accident story. The survivor, taken to Point Arno Hospital, has regained consciousness and given his name, Joe Gilliam. Hospital staff are already in touch with his wife."

"Joe Gilliam from the Allison house," I cried. "Then it's his friend, Kent O'Brien, who's dead. How awful!"

Even the boys were silent as we took in the news about our neighbors. The rest of the evening All of us were edgy the rest of the evening. The children snapped at one another. Ted paced back and forth in the living room before stepping out to the rain-spattered porch. Lew joined him while I tried to make light conversation with a nervous Lora.

"Fetus active tonight?" I asked.

Lora shook her head and said, "Not tonight. I just feel as if

I'm carrying a ton of lead."

By the time we were settled in our beds, the storm was raging around our house and pelting the windows with sheets of rain. Too restless to sleep I tried to read, but all I could think of were Joe and the dead man, Kent. Suppose they had left their windows open at the house. The floor would be soaked. Maybe they had a dog they forgot to feed. Slipping back into bed, I poked an almost-asleep Ted, and whispered, "We'd better make sure the Allison house is all right tomorrow."

"Sure, sure. Just let me sleep," he grumbled and turned over on his side.

Some time in the night the storm moved inland. When I climbed out of bed, the sun was breaking through the clouds and promising a clear day. On my way to the shower, I got a whiff of coffee brewing. Of course! Son Lew remembered that I liked my early morning coffee. When I emerged from the bathroom, Lew was standing by our bedroom door holding a cup of steaming brew for me.

"Thanks. Just what I needed," I said, taking a sip of the hot drink.

"Join me on the porch," he whispered. "We need to talk."

While I slipped into my jeans and T-shirt and gave my hair a few quick brushes, I fretted over what Lew had in mind. "Only one way to find out," I muttered to the sleeping cat blocking my way to the porch.

Lew and I sat nursing our coffee and making light conversation for a few minutes before he said, "Mom, I'm concerned for you and Dad up here."

"Why? We're a lot safer than you folks down in the city. We don't even lock doors up here."

"Safe? The nearest hospital is twenty miles away. Telephone lines go down frequently. Dad's ticker isn't strong."

"We're not so helpless as you imagine. Sure the telephone lines go down once in a while, but we can always walk to a neighbor for help." I raised my hand to stop Lew from protesting. "And Harry Burns, who is only three miles down the road, has offered to fly us out of here in an emergency."

"God! Only three miles down the road. A real help if you've broken your leg and Dad's had a heart attack."

Reaching over and taking his hand, I said, "What's really bothering you, Lew?"

He hesitated before answering. "I've heard rumors that there is gang action in this remote area. That road accident yesterday may be a result of such activity."

"Nonsense. The pickup was probably speeding on that narrow road and tried to pass too close to the panel truck."

"Or else the pickup driver deliberately rammed the panel truck," Lew said. "Why did the driver run away from the scene of the accident? He may be a hired killer. He may have a record."

Could Lew be right? I tried to keep from shaking at Lew's suggestion. While I sat in silence digesting these dreadful thoughts, Will and Tom pushed open the screen door and joined us. Tom needed his shoes tied, and Will had his sweater on wrong-side out.

"Can we go down to the beach?" Will asked, pulling his sweater back over his head.

"Sure. I'll go with you. You too, Mom," Lew said, giving me a warm smile.

"Wait until I get my jacket, boys," I said and tiptoed back into our bedroom.

The wooden risers were slippery from the rain, so I had to take extra precautions on my descent to the cove below the house. Since there was no fog today, I could see the large rocks of the sea lion rookery and hear the inhabitants bark their morning greetings to one another.

We spotted a couple of fishing boats headed out to sea. Maybe we could have a red snapper supper tonight. No, Eddie was treating us to dinner in town.

When I knelt down to look for a sand dollar, I saw a compass wedged under a rock. "Look at this, Lew What's a compass doing here among the sea anemones?"

Lew, who was pointing out some of the tiny swimmers in another pool to his boys, came over to examine my find. "This isn't a regular compass used by hikers or fishermen. It's a surveyor's compass." He turned it over in his hand. "What's there to survey down here?"

"Nothing I know about. Not in this isolated cove," I added, as fear crept into my voice. This wasn't casually dropped. It was tightly wedged under a rock. Worry lines etched Lew's face. "We'll take it back to the house. Maybe someone will be asking about it." Glancing at his watch, he said, "I'm hungry. Want me to make breakfast?"

"Yes," Will and Tom yelled. "Will you make pancakes, Dad?"

"If Grandma will let me," he said, winking at me.

"Gladly. I'll find the makings for you and squeeze oranges for juice."

When we reached the top of the cliff, we saw Lora and a now wide awakened sitting on the porch drinking coffee.

"More news about the accident," Ted said, getting up and coming over to kiss me. "They've found the body of a man answering the description of the one who fled the scene. He had a bullet in his back."

"And he had no identification on him," Lora added.

"What's going on around here?" I cried. "Two men run off the road, one killed in the accident, a third man shot and killed."

CHAPTER THREE

"Maybe there is something to those rumors about gang activity up here," Lew said.

"What gang activity? Ted asked. "Safest area in the state. Only job the sheriff's had to deal with recently is catching some poachers."

"He has a bigger one now, catching a murderer," Lew said. Turning to his dad, he added, "Better lock your doors from now on."

Ted shrugged his shoulders and said he'd think about it. "Right now all I have in mind is breakfast."

Over hot cakes we discussed the fatal accident and murder.

"Is there a Mrs. O'Brien?" Will asked before stuffing his mouth with another pancake.

"We'll soon know if she comes to claim the body," Ted said.

"She might ask to have him shipped home," I suggested. Getting up to pour more coffee, I added, "What about Joe Gilliam's wife? Could we do something to help her, while Joe is in the hospital?"

"Hey, let's wait until she gets here, Kay. No sense in sticking our noses in where they don't belong," Ted said, reaching for my hand.

Smarting from Ted's jibe, I was tempted to pour a few drops of hot coffee on his outstretched hand. Instead I said, "You folks can sit and talk all morning. I'm going to walk over to the Allison house and see what's happening. Might take along a mop to clean up any mess left by rain during last night's storm or a souvenir from a pet left in the house.

Squeezing my hand, Ted said, "Sorry for my remark. I'm going with you. Where's the mop? And we'll need a pail and some rags."

"We'll all go," Lora said. "Get your jackets, boys." As Will and Tom shoved back their chairs and streaked toward the bedroom, Lora gave me an impish grin. "Think I'd miss getting the scoop over at the Allison place?"

In a few minutes we were marching down the road carrying buckets, rags, mops and pet food. When we drew near the Allison house, we saw a car parked in the driveway. A man and woman, deep in conversation, were walking toward the house. At first they didn't hear or see us. At the crunch of our feet on the driveway, the man turned and stared at us.

While the man studied us in silence, the woman gave us a wan smile. Her cheeks were wet with tears.

Ted stepped forward during the awkward moment and said, "We're neighbors up the road. Pointing to the rest of us and our strange assortment of gear, he added. "We came by to offer you help. Thought you might need a mop up after the storm if you'd left the windows open. Nodding toward the can of pet food in Lora's hand, he said, "That's in case you have a hungry dog in the house."

The man muttered something I couldn't hear. Undeterred, Ted said, "Sorry I didn't introduce us. I'm Ted Roberts, and this is my wife, Kay, our daughter-in-law, Lora, and son, Lew." Checking the yelp over near the barbed wire fence, he added, "And those youngsters caught on your fence are grandsons, Will and Tom."

The man relaxed and smiled. "Mighty neighborly of you. I'm Frank Allen, and this is Mrs. O'Brien."

Of course he was Frank Allen, the squat little F.B.I. agent we'd first met five years ago. Didn't he recognize Ted and me? I shuddered remembering how vulnerable we were out on that lonely island where the murders took place. Crusty Frank Allen had

20

probably saved our lives. Now he couldn't remember us? Of course he was still playing his shadowy games as a sleuth! I pushed these thoughts aside, as I took Mrs. O'Brien's outstretched hand and said, "I am so sorry about your husband's death. Only yesterday he and Mr. Gilliam were having coffee with us at our place."

Her eyes filled with tears as she thanked us for our concern. Frank Allen eyed us with interest and, I thought, recognition; but he said nothing about our previous meeting. Instead he thanked us for our concern and assured us they had everything under control here at the house.

"No dog to feed. Dry floors. Perhaps we'll come over to your place, after we pick up Mr. O'Brien's things. Which house is it?"

"I'll draw you a map," Lew said, leaning up against a fence post and pulling a business card from his wallet. Pointing to the front of the card, he said, "That's my address in Center City, a long way for you to come for coffee today."

What a dumb statement, I thought to myself, as I watched Lew sketch the way to our cabin.

Handing it to Frank Allen, Lew said, "It's about a quarter of a mile from here on the other side of the road."

Seeing that we could do nothing at the Allison place and seeming to be in the way, we started back to our house. We stopped along the road to pluck a few berries off the vines. When Ted and I dropped behind the others, he leaned over and said, "Frank Allen! What's the F.B.I. doing up here?"

"You did recognize him. So did I. Why didn't he admit knowing us?"

"Well, we didn't greet him as an old friend either, did we?"

"As prickly as he was, I wouldn't call him a friend. More important, why is he here?" I said.

Before we could say anything more, Will and Tom jumped out of the nearby ditch and yelled, "We gotcha!" Will grabbed my hand and said, "We've been tracking you two bad guys. Pay up or go to jail "

"Caught by the law," I said. "How about a milk shake for payment?"

"Swell, with lots of chocolate."

Maybe Frank Allen and Mrs. O'Brien would drop over this afternoon or tomorrow.

While we snacked at lunch time, we turned on the TV for news. There was nothing about the accident or about the body found in the woods. As were started to turn off the TV, a reporter began interviewing a local resident who was irate over the threats he was receiving.

"This stranger was real nice and friendly on his first visit to my place. Asked about the neighborhood, how long I'd lived here. Did I know a good piece of land he could purchase. Those sorts of questions."

"You mentioned threats. When did they start?" the interviewer asked.

"About two weeks ago. This time the stranger brought another man along to visit us. Said he'd heard land prices were dropping in the area. Fear of earthquakes was the problem, he said. Looking around my lot, the first man added, "With all these trees, your place could go up in smoke before the volunteer firemen got their hoses out.""

"That's hardly a threat," the interviewer said.

"No, but two days later I had a note in my mailbox up at the post office saying, 'Fire's getting closer.'"

"What did you do?"

"Nothing. I threw it away, but I started to worry. This morning I found a can of gasoline sitting on top of my woodpile."

"Maybe someone in your family put it there to fill your power mower."

"I don't have a power mower, and no one besides the wife and me lives there." Pulling a torn piece of cardboard from his pants pocket, the resident said, "This was lying on the front seat of my car a few minutes ago."

The interviewer took the cardboard and read, "Next time there will be a lighted match in the gas can.' Wow, that is a threat!

Did you show it to the sheriff?"

"Sure. He says he'll look into it, but he's mighty busy right now, what with a body lying in the woods."

"A threat. A body. The truck accident. What is happening in your quiet town?" Lew said. "Wasn't the man being interviewed Abe Curtis?"

"Yes. He has a nice place just north of here," Ted said.

"Isn't that the only stretch of flat land on the ocean side for several miles?" I asked.

Ted nodded. Suddenly I remembered the newspaper article that mentioned a fusion reactor to extract hydrogen from sea water and combine it with helium-3 from moon rocks. I shook my head. I was imagining the impossible. No reactor would be built around here.

Deep in thought, I almost missed Lew's words. "What's the matter, Lora?"

I glanced at Lora, who hadn't taken part in our conversation. Her face was chalk white, and pain lines etched it. "It can't be the baby. It's too soon." Getting up and clutching her abdomen, she staggered toward the bedroom.

Lew rushed to her side. "Having contractions? I'll drive you to the hospital right now."

"Not yet. Let me lie down until they stop."

While Lew helped Lora to the bedroom, I cleared the lunch dishes and settled down with the crossword puzzle. The grandsons had gone with Ted to pick up the mail and a few groceries in town, so the house was blessedly quiet.

I was so absorbed in getting the right definition for verisimilitude that I didn't hear footsteps approaching. The knock on the screen door startled me before I heard Frank Allen say, "May we come in, Mrs. Roberts—Kay?"

As I unlocked the screen door, Mrs. O'Brien gave me a tentative smile and walked into the living room.

"Come on in and make yourselves comfortable while I make a fresh pot of coffee." Turning to Frank, I said, "So you did recognize us after all this time."

"Of course! How could I forget that strange little woman I met on the island case? It wasn't that long ago." Seeing Mrs. O'Brien's puzzled look, he went on to explain that he had met Ted and me a few years earlier on one of the Channel Islands off the Southern California coast.

"They were part of a team of specialists preparing that former naval base for its conversion to a new national park facility. I was called out there to break up an international smuggling ring, and I incidentally got a chance to meet these folks."

"And saved our lives," I added.

Before I could say more, Frank asked, "Do you ever hear from any of your team? That Japanese fellow, Marc Oku, wasn't it? Or that quick tempered Chilean, William something?"

"All of them regularly. That hot tempered Chilean, Bill Rodriquez, is now a family man. Owns his father's business and with his wife, Alice - remember her? - is raising a houseful of Rodriquez offspring."

Putting down my coffee cup, I said, "Enough reminiscing. You are still with the FBI, aren't you, Frank?"

"Until I hang up my badge and head for the rocking chair."

"OK, you didn't come here to chat. What's on your mind, Frank?"

"Always a gracious little lady," Frank said to Mrs. O'Brien. Giving me that interrogator's look, he began, "How did you happen to meet Kent O'Brien and Joe Gilliam, Kay?"

I told him about watching them come on shore in a raft while I was down at the beach looking for sand dollars in the tide pools. "They stopped by our house and had a cup of coffee with Ted and me on their way back to the Allison place. That was the only meeting I had with your husband and his friend, Mrs. O'Brien."

"Now you're wondering why I'm here, aren't you, Kay?" Frank asked as he directed a sharp glance at me from under his bushy eyebrows.

I nodded.

"Kent O'Brien was one of our most promising young agents

in the Bureau. Joe Gilliam is a ten-year veteran in the organization and one of Kent's instructors in our training school for candidates. Kent completed the program at the top of his class. Since his assignment to field duty he and Joe have worked as partners at Gilliam's request."

"Fine. Fine. But that doesn't explain your presence here and now."

He ducked his head and grinned. "I'd almost forgotten your impatience and sharp tongue. May I continue?"

"Sorry. Go on," I muttered.

"You may recall that I am one of the Bureau's trouble shooters assigned to follow up on initial investigations that indicate complicated criminal activity falling within the F.B.I.'s jurisdiction."

"Sounds like bureaucratic jargon to me."

Frank ignored my barb. "Kent and Joe were checking out an anonymous tip that such a situation was developing or was already in existence up here in these parts."

"Go on," I said, leaning forward in my chair.

"I hate to tell you, but that truck crash was no accident. It was a deliberate attempt to silence our two agents. It took Kent's life and almost killed Joe."

"How awful!" I gasped, and heard a sob escape from Mrs. O'Brien.

"Awful but true. Now Kay. Think carefully. Is there any detail you may think unimportant? Something Kent or Joe said to you? Anything you found down there on the beach? Any small thing that might be a clue for us?"

I sat still going over everything that had happened down on the beach or up here in our house. The compass. "I don't see any connection between what I found under a rock this morning and what happened to your two men, but I'll get it for you." I went to the mantel and brought him the compass.

Taking it from my hand and fingering it, he said, "It's a surveyor's compass. What is there to survey down in the inlet?"

I shrugged my shoulders.

"May I keep it?"

I nodded.

"Is there any piece of flat land on the ocean side of the road?"

"Abe Curtis' place just north of us," I said.

"Abe Curtis. Isn't he the man they interviewed on TV? The one who said he's being threatened?"

"Yes. Abe Curtis. Do you think someone was surveying his property without his permission?" I asked.

"Can't say," Frank answered and pocketed the compass. "Time we went back to the coroner's office, Janet. They should be finished with the autopsy by now."

I saw Mrs. O'Brien wince at his words. Tears sprang to her eyes when she thanked me for talking about her husband with her and Frank.

As Frank took Mrs. O'Brien's arm and led her down the steps, he said, "I'm sorry to miss Ted. How's his ticker?"

"He hasn't had any trouble since he retired. Amazing that you remembered that detail about his heart."

"Shall I tell you what you were wearing the first time I met you?"

I laughed and said, "Spare me."

"Although Janet and one of our agents will probably leave with Kent's body this afternoon, I'll stay around a while. Mind if I drop in to visit with you and Ted?"

"And pick our brains," I said. "Sure. Come any time. By the way, is there anything I can do for Mrs. Gilliam?"

"I'll let you know. Oh, good. Ted's turning in at the driveway. I'll have a few words with him. Come on, Janet."

While I stood on the porch watching Ted greet Frank and Mrs. O'Brien, I heard the screen door close and turned to see a worried Lew.

"Where's the nearest hospital? Point Arno? Lora's in a bad way."

CHAPTER FOUR

"Oh, no! The baby?" I cried and rushed into the house. Turning back to Lew, who was right on my heels, I said, "Sorry, son. Yes. Point Arno. Better phone the hospital and tell them we're coming."

"What's the number?"

"It's on the wall by the phone. Be about forty-five minutes," I added, hurrying to Lora.

She was bent over with pain, when I reached the bedside. Sweat poured down her face. I held her until the contraction passed.

"Thanks, Mom," she said, as she lay back down and closed her eyes. "Go with me, please."

I squeezed her hand and said, "I'll be with you." Grabbing a few things for her - tooth brush, makeup kit, warm robe - stuffed them into a canvas bag lying on the floor. Lew and I almost collided when he dashed into the room to say the hospital staff were waiting for us.

He carried Lora to the car, while I ran ahead with the bag to tell Ted where we were going. He and Frank were still reminiscing at the top of the lane. I felt sorry for Mrs. O'Brien having to stand and listen to stories about people she'd never met. At least it kept her mind off her loss for a few minutes. I was kissing Ted goodbye when

Lew braked beside me and waited for me to jump in the

back seat.

"I'll call you from the hospital," I yelled to Ted through the open window, as Lew gunned the motor and headed for the highway.

Lora made little moaning noises in the front seat. Lew reached over and took her clenched fist. "Hang in there, Lora girl," he murmured.

I leaned forward and rubbed her tense shoulders.

We crawled along the narrow twisting highway, dodging bicyclists and hikers. When we came to Abe Curtis' place, I craned my neck, looking for strangers lurking about the premises. I saw no one.

When the road snaked down toward an inlet, I watched fishing boats bobbing in the surf. There were a few hardy souls sunning themselves, while children played on the pebbly beach.

Now as we drove, we were shut off from the sea by a column of trees. A dog loped along the side of the road ahead of us and stopped to observe us as we passed him. He didn't even bother to bark. When we again saw the ocean, wisps of fog were moving landward. Would we be fog-bound on our return to our house?

Although we had been on the road less than an hour, it seemed much longer before we pulled into an emergency parking space in front of the hospital. Lora had drifted off to sleep after her last contraction but roused as soon as the car stopped. I saw an attendant pushing a wheelchair down the ramp toward us, as Lew switched off the engine and opened the car door for Lora. When the chair's brake was secured, he lifted her into the wheelchair and rolled the chair into the hospital. I grabbed Lora's bag and followed Lew and the attendant to the admittance desk where Lew turned his attention to filling out forms while the attendant and I made our way to the room assigned to Lora.

We were helping Lora undress and put on a hospital gown when we heard the intercom announce, "Paging Dr. Long to Room 112. Mrs. Roberts has arrived." Lora cried out as her pain intensified. "It was never this bad, Mom," she gasped between contractions. What's wrong?"

Before I could answer, I was brushed aside by a white coated doctor who ordered me out of the way. While I moved aside, a nurse ran into the room to assist him. When he raised his head after examining Lora he said to me, "Sorry, ma'am for my rudeness. You her mother?

"No, her mother-in-law. Can you save the baby?"

Without answering, he asked, "Where's her husband?"

"Here, Doctor," Lew said, coming in and closing the door. "Is she going to be all right?"

A troubled look crossed Dr. Long's face, as he motioned to Lew and me to follow him our of the room. As soon as the door closed, he asked, "How long has she been in labor?"

"At least three hours, but it's too early for the baby to come," I said.

Ignoring me, Dr. Long said, "She's not going to make it, Mr. Roberts, if we don't take the fetus now. Your wife's too weak from internal hemorrhaging to try for a normal birth." He hesitated before adding, "I can feel no movement of the fetus. It may be dead."

While I shuddered at these harsh words, Lew cried out, "What are you waiting for? I'll sign the papers. Just hurry."

"I'll do my best to save both of them," Dr. Long said, giving Lew a warm smile. Returning to the room, he ordered the nurse to prepare Mrs. Roberts for surgery.

While Lew signed some more papers and then followed Lora's gurney to the operating room, I sank down on a cushioned chair in the waiting room. I was numb with grief. Laura had carried this baby for six months and I already thought of him as our third grandchild. How long had Lora been hurting? What would we tell the boys, Will and Tom?

I roused when two scruffy looking men walked past me and settled in chairs near me. The one speaking almost fell over my outstretched feet as he said, "Dummy, don't you know poison ivy when you see it?"

"What do you think I am, a country boy?" the other replied. Glaring at his companion, he added, "A lot of help you were, standing there while I crawled around looking for the marker."

In spite of tripping over me, they finally seemed to notice my presence for the first time and stopped speaking.Marker? Were they surveyors? I thought about the surveyor's compass I'd given Frank Allen. Trying not to connect these two men with the compass, I said, "Sorry about your poison ivy. It's all over the place in these parts."

The first man smiled, revealing a chipped front tooth. "Tell this big baby that he'll live."

"Yes, but it will be uncomfortable for several days. They did give you something for it here, didn't they?" I asked the man with the poison ivy.

The patient nodded and replied, "If they ever fill the prescription." He writhed in the chair and complained, "I itch all over. Several days, you say? I can't stand it." Peering down the hall, he saw a nurse approaching with a package. "Well, finally," he muttered, and held out his hand for the parcel she was carrying.

Without a word of thanks or waiting for the instructions she started to give him, he stumbled toward the exit.

"A real clod, my buddy," Chipped Tooth said to the nurse as he followed the other man toward the door.

The nurse shrugged her shoulders and walked back to the desk.

While I sat alone, I tried to think what to say to Lew who should be along in a few minutes. No soothing words came to mind. Instead, as soon as I saw him, I began to cry. I sniffled and reached in my purse for a tissue. Lew pulled a clean handkerchief out of his shirt pocket and handed it to me before dropping on the couch beside me.

We were still sitting in silence when Dr. Long came to talk with Lew. "As I feared, the fetus was already dead. All we could do was to remove it from the birth canal but we managed to save your wife, Mr. Roberts. Another few days of her internal hemorrhaging, and we might have lost her."

"Oh, my God! Is she going to be all right?" Lew asked.

"Yes, but it will take time. She had a condition we doctors

call by a fancy name, abruption placentae or separation of the placenta. Among other symptoms it brings abdominal pain, irritation of the uterus and hemorrhaging. She will heal physically and emotionally in time.." Dr. Long studied Lew's sad face before he continued. "You do have other children, don't you?"

"Two boys," Lew said. Giving me an agonized look, he said, "God. What am I going to tell them?"

Before I could answer Dr. Long said, "The truth. This little one was not meant to come into your family. One fact you may not want to share with your sons. The fetus they were already calling their brother had no eyes."

My heart ached for Lew. Dr. Long continued to speak. "You and your wife can have more children if you wish. It might be a good idea for her to get pregnant as soon as she is healed from the surgery."

Getting up, he shook Lew's hand and said, "I'll keep her here for a couple of days to make sure there are no complications."

Grinning at me, Dr. Long said, "I should have acknowledged you sooner, but my mind was on the patient. I can see that your son is the spitting image of you. Take care of him." Looking down the hall, he added to Lew, "They will be wheeling your wife back into her room in a little while, but she will be asleep for at least another hour. Why don't you two get a bite to eat while you're waiting?"

"Any suggestions?" I asked.

"There's a good restaurant a block up the street, or you can suffer through our cafeteria fare. Oh, here she comes now," Dr. Long said, as an attendant pushed a gurney toward us.

Lew rushed over and took Lora's limp hand and accompanied his sleeping wife into her room. Dr. Long followed them and closed the door. As soon as I was alone, I walked down the hall to the public telephone and dialed Ted.

I sobbed, as I said, "She lost the baby, but she is going to be all right. Do you want to wait for Lew to tell the boys?"

"Yes, I'll leave that up to him. How is he taking it? I can hear what it's doing to you." His warm, wonderful voice made me want to wrap myself in his protective arms.

Stifling a sob, I told him we'd both be all right. Our only concern was for Lora. Remembering that I had a hungry husband and two starving grandsons at home, I said, "Why don't you take Tom and Will out for hamburgers tonight? Lew and I'll get back to the house some time this evening."

"Be careful in the fog. I hear it's rolling in heavy up north," Ted said and added before hanging up, "I love you."

I stopped by the admittance desk and asked about Joe Gilliam. The nurse reported that he was stabile but could have no visitors.

Lew was coming out of Lora's room when I returned. "Let's try that restaurant Dr. Long mentioned," Lew said, taking my arm and guiding me toward the exit. "This will give Lora time to rest after her ordeal."

The lilies we always call naked ladies formed a border of dancing girls along the sidewalk. Their lavender and pink blossoms were in full bloom. Orange, red and yellow nasturtiums nodded to us from their beds beside the wooden porches. Pots of bright red geraniums hung from the eaves on several porches. Seeing all this serene beauty helped ease the sense of loss I was experiencing.

Neither of us was hungry, and we merely picked at our food. It may have been delicious, but we'd never have known. When we returned to the hospital, Lora was awake.

She smiled her greeting and said, "Glad you didn't come sooner. I managed to up chuck my dinner. Got a cracker I can gnaw on at bedtime?"

"Nope, but I'll get you a whole package from the cafeteria if you want it. Or I'll waylay a nurse and ask for a tray for you," he said, leaning down and giving her a kiss before he left the room.

Their love for each other was as strong as Ted's and mine. I hoped our son, Eddie, would some day find such a loving, caring partner. While these thoughts were going through my mind, Lora held out her hand to me and said, "Thanks, Mom, for being here. I needed both of you."

Brushing a lock of her dark brown hair out of her eyes, I

said, "I wouldn't be anywhere else if you wanted me. And don't worry about Will and Tom. Dad's treating them to hamburgers for supper. They'll convince him they need milkshakes to wash down the burgers."

"The boys! Who is going to tell them?" she asked.

"I am," Lew said, coming back into the room with a nurse and a tray of food. "Unless Dad's already told them."

"I shook my head and said, "He's leaving that up to you, Lew. You will know what's best to tell them."

I saw relief in Lew's face at my words before he turned to the nurse holding the tray. "Not lobster thermidor, but Nurse Abbie managed to get you a tuna sandwich and a cup of tea."

"Great!" Lora said, reaching out for the tray. "Mmmm. Tuna sandwich and a dish of Jell-O along with the tea. Thanks, Nurse Abbie," she said before tucking the napkin into her lap and biting into the sandwich.

"Enjoy," I said, kissing her good night before stepping out into the hall to wait for Lew.

Even though it was only eight o'clock, the fog had darkened the landscape so that we had to inch our way along the coast road back to our house. We talked very little as we concentrated on watching for deer crossing the highway. It was almost nine thirty when we turned into our driveway. I saw the flutter of our living room curtain and two little faces in the window. Will and Tom were peering out into the night.

Before Lew had turned off the engine, the door opened and the boys ran out to greet us. Ted followed at a slower pace. I hoped his heart was not giving him trouble again, but maybe he was just exhausted from keeping up with two lively boys.

"Where's Mamma," Tom cried. "Did she bring our baby brother home?"

"She's going to sleep at the hospital tonight. Come in and I'll tell you about it," Lew said, putting his arms around his sons and leading them into their bedroom.

While Lew talked with the boys, I told Ted what had happened at the hospital. "Dr. Long assured Lew that he and Lora can have more children if they wish." I stopped talking when the bedroom door opened. Tom ran in and crawled into my lap.

Burying his head in the crook of my arm, he said between sobs, "Our baby brother is dead, Grandma."

"I know," I said and rocked him in my lap. When I looked over at Will standing next to his father, I saw tears trickling down his cheeks. Motioning for him to come to me, I said, "It's all right to cry, Will." Without a word he came over and put his arms around me, and I felt his tears dampening my neck.

CHAPTER FIVE

Ted tried to lighten the atmosphere by suggesting a game we could all play, but he had no takers. Before long the five of us were tucked in our beds for the night.

My first thoughts when I awakened the next morning, Thursday, were of Lora. Lew planned to drive to Point Arno after breakfast to visit her. "I hope he takes the boys with him," I said to Ted, who was riding our stationary bicycle in the bedroom.

"Be good for him and the boys to make a day of it. Visit Lora. Go out to the lighthouse and climb up those stairs to the lookout windows. I'll suggest it at breakfast." Getting off the bicycle, he added, "I wish I could still climb up those stairs."

Pulling on my jeans, I said, "Forget the stairs. You and I have a special guy coming this afternoon. Remember?"

"The one and only - Eddie! Didn't he write that he's taking us out to dinner?"

I nodded and said, "Remember last time he was here? I can still see him stalking that porcupine and focusing his camera on the fellow. He kept clear of those quills but somehow managed to rouse the wrong end of a skunk."

"How could I ever forget that stink?" Ted said, and laughed.

When we walked into the kitchen, Lew and the boys were lining up the cereal boxes and putting bowls on the table. When they finished, Tom went to the refrigerator, and after a struggle,

35

brought a gallon of milk to the table. Big brother Will stuck a couple of pieces of bread in the toaster and brought over the butter for toast. The three of them must have gone berry picking while we slept because Lew returned to his job of washing the berries and putting them in my best flowered bowl.

"Morning, folks. What will it be? Shredded wheat, raisin bran, corn flakes, Cheerios?" six-footer Lew asked, leaning down to kiss me.

"Mmm, even the shredded wheat smells good today," Ted said, bending over the box and sniffing its contents. "Thanks, Tom," he said, relieving his grandson of the milk, which was teetering on the edge of the table. "What are your plans for the day?"

"See Mamma," Tom yelled.

"Right. As soon as we've finished breakfast, brushed our teeth and made up our beds, we'll be off to the hospital, guys." Turning to us, he said, "Lora wants a few more things - a night gown and slippers. You took her makeup kit in yesterday, didn't you, Mom?"

I nodded.

"Anything else we should take?"

"I'll send along a couple of mysteries to while away her time," I said.

"I'll show her the snake skin I found yesterday," Will said, pulling this treasure out of his pocket.

"That will make her day," Lew said and grinned.

"Can I take one of my games along, Dad?" Tom asked.

"Sure. Anything else?"

"Just a suggestion from me," Ted said. "Why don't the three of you make a day of it? Go to the lighthouse. Count the seals playing right next to the lighthouse. Have a picnic in the city park."

"I'll pack a lunch for you," I said, getting up and reaching for the peanut butter.

While we ate breakfast and I put together a lunch for them, Ted regaled us with stories about the lighthouse. "Nowadays people can sometimes stay overnight there. Hear the wind howl on stormy nights and pretend that they are the lighthouse keepers. Think of climbing all those stairs every night to light the beacon. Then, in the daytime, check the light and clean all those windows up there."

"Can we light the lamp?" Will asked.

"Not any more. It's all automated. But you can hear the creaking of the equipment and watch the sea lions playing off the coast. Look way out to sea and search for an oil tanker moving on the horizon."

"Ooh, let's go," Will said, giving his brother a jab in the arm. "First one through his chores gets to sit by the window."

As Ted's singing clock chimed nine o'clock, we waved Lew and the boys on their way to Point Arno with a reminder to give Lora our love.

Ted had slipped a few cartoons into the bag of goodies for Lora. I hoped she would appreciate Will's snake skin.

The dust raised by Lew's car was still settling when I saw Frank Allen turn into our driveway. "Darn. I won't have time for my trampoline this morning," I muttered to myself.

Parking his van, Frank leaned out the window and said, "Can you spare a few minutes for talk?"

"Sure. Come on in and tell us the latest news," Ted said.

Frank grinned and said, "You know I rarely bring news, good or bad. I come only to get information." Glancing at me, he said, "I hear you were at the hospital yesterday. How is your daughter-in-law?"

"Just swell after losing her baby. What's on your mind?"

Frank ignored my first remark. "Your visit to the hospital yesterday. Did you see or talk with anyone other than your daughter-in-law and the staff there?"

"Only a couple of men. One was whining about his poison ivy. He didn't even have the courtesy to thank the person who brought him his prescription. The other one, with a chipped front tooth, tripped over my feet on his way to a chair near me. He was anything but kind to his buddy. Called him a dummy and a baby.

Why do you ask?"

"Because they were snooping around the hospital. They stopped at the desk and asked to see Joe Gilliam. They claimed to be friends of his."

"They didn't get to see him, did they? I asked about Mr. Gilliam and was told he couldn't have visitors."

"That's right. No one except his wife, Julia, and law enforcement personnel who have clearance. When these characters you describe found they couldn't wheedle their way in to see Joe, they began to threaten the nurse on duty. Fortunately, Dr. Long came by at that moment and sent them packing." Frank hesitated before continuing. "At least he thought he had discouraged them. Later they were found hanging around outside Joe's room by the guard who had just stepped outside for a smoke." Frank shifted in his chair, then said, "Tell me exactly what you heard these men say, when they were in the waiting room."

"It may mean nothing, but the one with the poison ivy was complaining, as you might expect. Let me try to remember his words. 'A lot of help you were, standing up there while I crawled around looking for the marker.'"

"That fits," Frank said.

"What do you mean?"

Frank grinned at me and said, "You know I like to keep secrets. Tell me. Did you notice any distinguishing marks on either man?"

Provoked by Frank, I tried to control my temper as I said, "I didn't check for tattoos, if that's what you mean. That's kind of personal, don't you think? The one with the poison ivy was pretty obvious—big red welts. The other man had a chipped front tooth. That's not much of a description for you, is it?"

"It's very good. With your keen powers of observation, we might be needing you in the F.B.I."

"You'd be my boss? Never!"

"Watch it, Kay. Frank is trying to gather facts," Ted said, putting his hand on my arm. Turning to Frank, he asked, "Did Mrs. O'Brien leave?"

Frank nodded and lowered his eyes. Could those be tears I saw on his face? When he looked up, he said, "The death of one of my men or women is the hardest thing I experience. Yet I know how much harder it is on the family."

The three of us were silent for a few minutes watching a blue jay tease a stray cat that had wandered across our lawn. I broke the silence by asking how Joe Gilliam was doing.

"That's the other thing I wanted to tell you. Joe would like to see you two, when you can get up to the hospital. I'll have a clearance waiting for you at the desk. And, oh yes, Julia, his wife is pretty lonesome. She's staying there in Point Arno. Here, I'll give you her address," Frank said, as he scribbled it on a torn piece of paper.

"We'll go up and visit him and his wife tomorrow," I said. Wonder what's on his mind."

"Only one way to find out," Frank said, getting up from his chair. "I'd better get along and hope something breaks on this case soon. If you see or hear anything out of the ordinary, call me at this number," he said, ripping off another corner of the torn sheet and writing the phone number down for us.

The rest of the day was quiet. Ted helped me make up the sofa bed for Eddie before taking off for his daily walk to pick up the mail and newspaper. For some reason I felt uneasy having Frank's telephone number. Scolding myself for my anxiety, I folded the slip of paper into the shape of a tiny bud and stuck it in among the blossoms of a bunch of artificial flowers the boys had made for Ted and me.

We listened to the news broadcast at noon but heard no mention of any new developments on the accident or murder. Instead of another interview with Abe Curtis over threats to his property, we were treated to a homey feature on raising three kinds of mushrooms.

"Big deal!" Ted grumbled, turning off the radio and handing me the daily newspaper open to my crossword puzzle.

I was searching my brain for the answer to the last clue in the puzzle when I heard a vehicle career into our driveway and pull

to a stop at the foot of our porch steps.
   "Hey, anybody home?" a man shouted.

CHAPTER SIX

"It's Eddie!" Ted cried, getting up from his chair and pushing open the screen door. "Come out and greet our son, Kay."

After giving his dad a bear hug, Eddie held out his arms to me. When I reached up to kiss him, he lifted me off the ground and said, "Remember how you used to scold and shake your finger at me, Mom? Now try it."

"I'm still boss, you big lug," I said, laughing and trying to pull his hair. "Put me down, so I can have a good look at you."

After giving me a chance to inspect him, Eddie reached into the back of his van and took out a couple of small canvas bags. "I'll leave most of my gear in here." Giving me a mischievous look, he held up one of the bags and said, "Dirty clothes. Just what you need."

"You know how to turn on the washer. Be my guest," I said, putting my arm around him, as we walked up the steps.

Over cold drinks we listened to Eddie tell about his latest assignment in Saudi Arabia. "I hope I never eat and breathe that much sand again. And the fleas! In spite of those annoyances I met wonderful people and took thousands of pictures of that magnificent land." Stopping in the midst of his story, he looked around and said, "Where are Lew and Lora and those little devils, Will and Tom?"

While Ted told him about Lora's losing the baby, I studied my son. He was the tallest member of the family. Six-three last time

41

we measured him. His rich brown hair was streaked with gray, a gift from my genes. A lock of it hung over his eyes as he talked. Thanks to his recent trip to the Middle East he was tanned. There were a few wrinkles around his merry brown eyes. My son with wrinkles? Impossible!

Catching me staring at him, he said, "Will I pass muster, ma'am?"

"Give me time to decide." Reaching over and squeezing his arm, I added, "It's so good to have you home. Can we keep you here while you're on this assignment?"

"You bet. You can't get rid of me until I finish this stint, unless you and Dad throw me out of the house." Digging into one of his bags, he brought out a large sheet of paper and said, "Want to see the game plan?"

Ted and I leaned down and studied the detailed sheet Eddie spread on the floor.

"I'm to find and photograph every kind of plant growing on the ocean front for a fifteen-mile stretch, which includes your place."

"Good. That will take forever," I said.

"Long enough for you to get tired of me," Eddie said.

Ted, ignoring our exchange, looked up and said, "Fascinating, but why did your company choose this area and limit it to the ocean side?"

Eddie shrugged his shoulders and replied, "I don't know. I just follow orders." Folding up the sheet of paper and sitting back in his chair, he said, "It's going to be a devil of a job getting from one inlet to the next and crawling almost perpendicularly in several spots. Want to suspend me by rope while I photograph, Dad?"

"Sure, I'll do the rope bit. We can practice our act behind the house." Giving a wistful sigh, he added, "It will make me feel useful again."

It hurt to hear Ted admit that retirement wasn't all he'd dreamed of. He'd never complained, as we settled here on the coast. He was studying the history of the Indians who had formerly lived here and the early years of the lumber industry. However, he had to wait days for books and manuscripts to arrive from the university to further his research. We'd have to get on the Internet to speed up his work.

Right now teaming up with Eddie might be just the stimulation he needed if it didn't give him another heart attack.

While Eddie's clothes sloshed away in the washing machine, the three of us walked down to our cove. The tide was in, so we couldn't examine tide pools. The incoming waves smashed against the big rocks and covered the smaller ones. Water ran up the beach on silent fingers and left a trail of foam and damp sand as it retreated and prepared for the next onslaught. In the distance we could see three fishing boats heading toward the inlet to the north of us.

On the horizon we made out the shape of a large ship. A tanker? A naval vessel? We couldn't tell from this distance.

The breeze had picked up while we stood mesmerized by the sea. When clouds momentarily covered the sun, I shivered and started back toward the steps.

"Had enough, Mom?" Eddie asked. Looking at his watch, he added, "It's almost dinner time. Where do you want me to take you to eat? My treat, remember."

Ted named a favorite restaurant of ours while we climbed back up the cliff. The wind was stronger and sharper as we neared the top. I was puffing by the time we reached even ground and walked the few yards to our cabin.

"Lew's back," Ted said. "Got something for him and the boys to eat, Kay?"

"Hey, you think I'm a piker? I'm taking all of us out to eat., even my charged up nephews," he said, as Will and Tom threw themselves at their uncle and hugged him.

I ran ahead to find out about Lora. Lew gave me a short report and promised to talk more about it later. "She's kind of blue today," he said, before hurrying to greet his brother.

While the men talked, I got the boys to wash up and change their clothes. I donned my one respectable suit and ran a comb through my tangled hair. I even added lipstick for the occasion.

When I came out of the bedroom, the men were chatting in the living room. On seeing me, Eddie cried, "Cinderella is dressed for the ball. May I have this dance?"

"Silly," I said as he whirled me around the room; and the boys clapped their appreciation.

Over dinner Lew told us more about Lora. "Dr. Long expects to release her tomorrow." He hesitated before going on. "However, she is suffering from depression over losing the baby. Doc says she will need all the loving attention we can give her for the next several weeks." Turning to Eddie, he said, "You'll be a tonic for her. She's always liked your sense of humor."

"I'll do my best to help her, big brother. She's a favorite of mine."

For a few minutes we ate in silence as we concentrated on the steaks Eddie insisted we order.

Will broke the silence by saying, "Mamma beat us at slap jack almost every game." He beamed as he added, "You should have seen her face when I gave her my snake skin."

Tom interrupted his brother and asked, "Uncle Eddie, have you been to the lighthouse? It's fun but kind of scary."

"Sure. Lots of times. Spotted a whale once when I was there." Putting down his napkin and getting up from his chair, he said, "Who would like to see pictures of camels, a desert snake having its dinner, children living in Saudi Arabia?"

"What's Saudi Arabia?" Tom asked.

"A big country like ours, except it has lots more sand than we do. Come on. Let's go home and meet those people and animals," Eddie said.

On the way home, Tom and Will were still muttering about what they might see in Uncle Eddie's pictures. Ted set up a screen for Eddie to show his slides. I was proud of our son as he took us on a colorful trip through Saudi Arabia. The boys were entranced by the snakes slithering in the sand and by the camel races.

Eddie closed his travelogue with a promise to teach Will and Tom a few words of Arabic. "That will impress your friends," he said as he gave each of them a pat on the rear and sent them off bed.

I fell asleep even before Ted came to bed and dreamed I was trying to mount a camel.

Some time around midnight Ted and I were jarred awake by a tremendous blast. Sitting up in bed, we tried to identify the sound. Was it a sonic boom? Thunder?

While we were reaching for our slippers and robes, we heard Will cry out, "Daddy, the sky's on fire!"

Rushing to our bedroom window we looked at the inferno to the north of us. Fire!

"My God, that's the Curtis place," Ted shouted. Rushing from the room he ran to the phone and dialed the fire department. Within minutes we heard cars racing toward the fire station. Soon we saw members of the voluntary crew clinging to the fire truck as it sped past our house. We heard the squeal of the brakes on the truck and the grinding of gears as it shifted into low and turned into Abe's place.

We ran back to our rooms and pulled on jeans and T-shirts. Grabbing my flashlight and a heavy jacket, I hurried along with the Ted and the others up to the highway. Here we were joined by a host of folks walking or biking toward Abe's place. There was a hum of conversation. No one knew what had happened. Was Abe all right? How about his wife, Alice?

"Remember that interview Abe gave the TV station?" one man remarked as we passed him on the road.

"Yeah. Something about a threat," another answered him.

When we walked through the open gate, we saw that the fire fighters were too late to save the house. Only the stone chimney remained intact. The ground around it still felt hot to the touch. In spite of this, the fire fighters had managed to stop the spread of the fire short of the tinder-dry trees and underbrush

There was nothing we could do but stare at the devastation. The fire fighters were spraying likely hot spots, hoping to catch any remaining burning bits that had exploded from the house. No one spoke. It was too terrible a sight. Gradually the crowd thinned. Only the acrid smell of the fire filled the air.

It was then that I spotted Alice, her hair in curlers and wearing a tattered bath robe. She was leaning against a tree and clutching her purse. Some people were clustered around her. She didn't respond, only moaned and weaved back and forth. While I watched, she seemed to notice those around her for the first time. As neighbors tried to comfort her, she let out a wail and sank to the ground. I pushed my way to her. Kneeling down, I cradled her head on my shoulder and listened to her cry uncontrollably.

"It's gone. Everything. Our life savings," she said, between fits of sobbing.

Finally the weeping subsided. A friend helped me lead Alice over to one of the few remaining grassy spots on the property. Exhausted from the ordeal, she fell into a troubled sleep, waking every few minutes and calling out to her husband, Abe.

I hadn't seen Abe. He was probably talking with the fire fighters. Maybe Ted was with him. I hadn't seen Ted since we had entered the property.

While I was searching for Ted, I bumped into Frank Allen, who was bent over and examining a piece of metal.

"Ouch," he said, before straightening up and turning to look at me. "I might have known you would be snooping around here." Kneeling down on the warm earth, he pulled me down beside him and pointed to the metal object he had been studying.

"Know what it is?" he asked me.

I shook my head and started to reach for it.

He slapped my hand and said, "Don't touch it with your bare hand. Here, take one of my gloves."

CHAPTER SEVEN

Although peeved by his words, I knew he was correct. I might be touching a valuable clue which was also still too hot to pick up. Curbing my tongue, I replied, "It looks like part of a tin can. What harm could an old tomato can be?"

"You really are slow. Where's the rest of it? Here, smell it," he said pushing the metal toward me. I scooted over closer to him and bent down toward the metal as he asked, "Notice anything?"

"It smells like the Fourth of July. Firecrackers?" Staring at him, I asked, "Dynamite?"

Nodding, he said, "Probably. The can could have exploded and sent shards all over the place. Care to crawl around with me?"

"I haven't been asked to go crawling since I was a baby," I said. "Got an extra pair of gloves?"

"No, we'll share."

"Fun night out with the F.B.I.," I murmured.

He ignored my silliness and said, "Two things we'll be looking for more pieces of tin and, if we're lucky, gasoline-soaked rags. Maybe a defective stick of dynamite."

When I switched on my flash light, he hissed, "Turn that thing toward the ground, not on my face." When I obliged and apologized, he added,

"Watch out for snakes. They like the warm ground."

47

"Thanks for those comforting words," I said and began inching my way along the ground, feeling its heat even through the glove Frank had given me. Each time I shifted my weight to move on, I ran my light close to the ground to make sure I wasn't putting my hand or knee on a slithering serpent.

We spent the next hour down on our knees probing for clues. In that time we collected several bits of metal - possibly from an exploded can or cans and put them in a plastic bag Frank hung around his neck. I had just spotted a rag, when my view was cut off by a pair of legs. Ted! My flash light shone on his rolled up jeans.

"What are you two clowns doing?" he asked. "I've been looking all over for you, Kay."

"Cut out the humor, Ted," I said, pushing him out of the way. "Help Frank and me look for pieces of tin or a wad of rag."

Groaning, Ted dropped down on his knees and began to feel his way through the soot and burned pine cones while I told him what Frank suspected.

A flash of light blinded me for a second. Shielding my eyes, I looked up to see our son, Eddie, with his camera focused on me.

"You look great, Mom, with that smudge over your left eye," he said. "While hunting for you and Dad, I've been scouting the layout with camera shots."

"I didn't see you carrying your camera out of the house," I said.

"Not very observant, Mom. A camera freak doesn't go anywhere without his other set of eyes."

Eddie wheeled around when Frank Allen barked, "Watch where you're stepping!"

I heard a low chuckle and saw Ted get to his feet. "That's right, son. You may be destroying a clue. This tactful fellow who startled you is Frank Allen, F.B.I."

Dropping a piece of metal out of his gloved left hand into the bag, Frank shook hands with Eddie and said, "Sorry I snapped at you. Just don't want to destroy any evidence we might find here tonight."

"Evidence? F.B.I. What's going on here?" Eddie asked.

Frank didn't bother to answer Eddie's questions. Instead, he pointed to Eddie's camera and said, "Here, take a picture of this piece of dynamite I put in my bag."

Seconds later I saw a flash from the camera.

"Thanks," Frank said. "Will you give me copies of everything you've photographed tonight?" Before Eddie could reply, Frank added, "Stay close to me and get a shot of anything I think may be useful in our investigation."

"You suspect arson, don't you?" Not waiting for an answer, Eddie said, "If so, come over near the house, and I'll show you a piece of fuse next to the chimney."

Frank jumped to his feet and followed Eddie while Ted dropped beside me. We continued our crawl, adding to our pile of bits and pieces I stuck in the protective plastic bag Frank had given me.

The members of the fire department were rolling up their hoses after a final wetting down of the ground and checking for any smoldering embers among the trees and cones on the ground at the edge of the clearing when I heard familiar cries.

"Grandma. Grandpa. Where are you?"

"Over here, boys," I answered and turned the flash light on Ted and me. When Will stumbled against me, I dropped the flash light and folded him in my arms. I looked over and saw Ted sitting upright on the ground and hugging Tom.

"Thank goodness, you two are safe," Lew said, standing between us. Looking down at his sleepy sons, he added, "They've been worried about you and have been pleading for all of us to go home. Any reason to stay longer?"

"Not unless old Frank still needs us," Ted said, handing Tom to Lew and slowly getting to his feet. "Help your grandmother, Will. Her knees are probably as stiff as mine from creeping along the ground for hours."

"It just seems like hours," I said, accepting Will's help and then dusting off my smudged hands. "Enough of this. As soon as I give this bag of evidence to Frank, let's go home."

"I'll take it," Frank's voice growled near me before he

relieved me of the plastic bag.

Eddie was somewhere on the property and might not return to our place until dawn. We joined the few departing stragglers who had stayed around after the fire truck left as we headed for the highway and home. The fire chief had taken Abe and Alice Curtis with him for the rest of the night.

While Lew tucked Will and Tom into bed, I made cocoa for him, Ted and me. The three of us were too keyed up to sleep. Even though a light fog hung over the ocean, we took our drinks and sat on the porch talking.

"Both Frank and Eddie suspect arson," I said. "Those scattered pieces of tin sure look suspicious."

"I wonder whether those men who threatened Abe were around there last night?" Ted said.

"I didn't see any strangers, but that doesn't mean anything as so many people were milling around in the dark," Lew said.

"Lucky there was fog instead of wind. In a strong wind ours might have been the next place to go up in smoke," Ted reminded us.

Early morning light was filtering through the trees when we heard Eddie crunch his way along the driveway. Surprised but pleased to see us, he plopped down on the top step and leaned against the porch railing. "It's arson, all right," he said, slurping the hot cocoa I poured for him.

"Has the county sheriff arrived?" Ted asked.

"No, but his deputy was in contact with him throughout the night. He should get over here from Ukiah later this morning." Stretching and giving a big yawn, Eddie stood up and started toward the living room. "I gotta get some shut-eye. Hope I can sleep until noon."

Maybe Eddie could sleep until noon, but there wasn't much chance for Lew whose two lively boys usually woke up with the dawn.

When I awakened later in the morning, the fog that had hung over the coast during the night was almost gone. The sun promised us a clear day. Sometimes it didn't live up to its promises.

Lew and the boys were finishing breakfast and preparing to drive to Point Arno Hospital as I walked into the kitchen.

"Here, Mom," Lew said, handing me a cup of coffee. This will open your eyes and start the brain cells working."

"Thanks," I mumbled and braced myself for hugs from Will and Tom. I wondered how they could be so full of pep after only a few hours of sleep.

Looking over at Lew, I said, "Mind if I tag along to Point Arno? I want to talk with Joe Gilliam and visit his wife, Julia.

"Glad for your company," Lew said. "As soon as we check Lora out of the hospital, I'll take the family to lunch. That will give you time to see the Gilliams, won't it?"

"Plenty of time. I might drop into the cafeteria and snag a sandwich for my lunch if it's a short visit," I said.

After cleaning up the breakfast dishes and making the beds, we tiptoed down the steps toward Lew's car. "Darn. I forgot to leave a message for Ted, " I said and ran back into the house

No need for a note. I almost bumped into Ted yawning his way out of our bedroom.

"Where are you off to this morning?" he asked.

"Point Arno," I said. "I'm going to visit the Gilliams. After lunch we may bring Lora back with us. See you later," I added and kissed him goodbye.

As we pulled out of our driveway onto the highway, Lew said to the boys, "There's a carnival at Point Arno. Do you want to go there?"

"Oh, boy!" Tom cried. "Can I ride on the Ferris wheel?"

"I want to ride something real dangerous, not a sissy ride," Will said.

"We'll check out the place after we see your mother and may be able to bring her with us," Lew promised.

I interrupted Lew's telling the boys about today's plans by asking whether Lew had tucked in an extra sweater for Lora.

He nodded and went on with the day's plans.

I rolled down the window to let the cool salt air blow across my face. While Lew concentrated on avoiding a line of bicyclists puffing up the hill, I settled back to enjoy the coastal scenery. I still found the view fascinating after five years in this place.

The night's ordeal had taken its toll on Will and Tom who curled up in the back seat and fell asleep.

While I soaked up the beauty of land and sea, I thought about the Gilliams. Joe wanted to see both Ted and me. Why? Ted should have gone with me. Maybe we'd go back together later today. We ought to invite Julia Gilliam to stay with us. Point Arno could be a lonely place, unless you liked to fish or play bingo.

It was almost noon that Friday, when we parked at the hospital. The boys awoke the minute we stopped and leaped out of the car. After rolling on the grass and pummeling each other, they raced up the hospital steps. Lew yelled at them to wait for him.

As Lew and I walked at a more leisurely pace up the hospital steps, he looked at his watch and said, "We'll meet you here at the front in about an hour and a half. One thirty ok?"

"Fine. Give my love to Lora."

The boys were pulling their dad along the corridor toward their mother's room, when I stepped up to the admissions desk to ask for Joe.

Gilliam's room number. Strange, there was no attendant. I rang the bell on the counter. No response. Irritated by the delay, I started down the hall, hoping to find help. I saw a nurse come out of a room and shut the door. Instead of coming toward me, she went in the opposite direction. I ran to catch up with her.

"Nurse," I called after her retreating figure.

She turned and said, "May I help you?"

Of course she could help me. Why would I be chasing her, if I didn't want help? Instead of voicing these thoughts, I said, "I'm looking for Joe Gilliam's room. No one was at the admissions desk for me to ask."

Her face paled under her light makeup, and her hands began to shake as she said, "Who are you?"

"Mrs. Roberts. Kay Roberts. Mr. Gilliam asked to see my husband, Ted, and me; but Ted wasn't ready to drive up with me," I babbled, confused by the nurse's response.

"May I see some identification?" she said.

"Identification? Sure," I said and began rummaging in my purse. I pulled out my driver's license and handed it to her.

She studied it and looked at me. A tired smile played across her face as she returned the driver's license. "I'm sorry I had to question you, Mrs. Roberts. Clearance came through for you last night. Come back to the desk with me and sign the visitors' register."

"Sign in? Can't you just tell me the room number? I can find my way."

"I'll take you after you sign in," she said and opened the register for me. She stood beside me and watched me sign. Satisfied with my signature, she slipped the book into a drawer and said, "This way, Mrs. Roberts."

Thoroughly confused by this time, I followed her down the hall. When she stopped beside a closed door and knocked, I asked, "Is something wrong with Mr. Gilliam?"

She didn't answer. She put her head against the door and listened. I heard a voice say, "Who is it?"

"Annabelle," she answered. There was a click in the lock. The nurse-Annabelle-turned the knob and stepped in, closing the door behind her. Bewildered, I stood and stared at the closed door. In less than a minute she opened the door and let me in.

The first thing I noticed were people standing around a bed in the middle of the room. A well-dressed, middle-aged woman with graying brunette hair and a rather pretty but drawn face was weeping. A tall dark-haired, huskily built man with a ruddy complexion and bright blue eyes stood beside her. His forest green uniform and the shield-shaped shoulder patch and badge on his blouse identified him as the local sheriff. A white-jacketed man turned from the bed and approached the woman.

"Dr. Long!" I whispered to myself. "What is going on here?"

Taking the woman's hand, Dr. Long said, "Your husband's going to make it, Mrs. Gilliam."

The circle around the bed broke apart when the doctor led

Mrs. Gilliam over to the bedside. At that moment I got a glimpse of a comatose Joe Gilliam.

CHAPTER EIGHT

I shuddered as I stared at the inert form on the bed. Maybe I should step out of the room and leave his wife alone with her fears. I felt a tap on my shoulder and looked into the smiling eyes of the nurse, Annabelle.

She whispered, "Come meet Mrs. Gilliam. She needs the comfort of a woman."

As we walked toward the bed, I watched Gilliam's wife touch her husband's arm.

"Joe," she said in a soft voice, "Can you hear me?"

Joe's eyes flickered, then opened. In spite of being hampered by the IV connected to his arm, he searched and found her hand. She stood by his bedside caressing his forehead with her free hand. Suddenly his hand went limp.

"It's all right, Mrs. Gilliam," Dr. Long said.

"Joe has just drifted off to sleep. He's going to make it, but now he needs his rest."

Turning toward me, Dr. Long added, "Why don't you go along with Mrs. Roberts and have a bite to eat?"

Tears streaked Mrs. Gilliam's face as she leaned over and kissed her husband. "See you later, fighter," she murmured, before moving away from the bed and following Dr. Long toward me.

After a brief introduction, the doctor left us and returned to his patient. When she turned toward the closed door, I took her arm and led her out of the room and down the hall toward the cafeteria. "We both need a cup of coffee, and maybe you'll be hungry enough to tackle a sandwich or a bowl of soup," I said. When she gave me a tentative smile, I added, "Let's not be so formal. Just call me Kay, and what may I call you?"

"Julia. I was named for Mother's favorite sister."

I could feel Julia relax as she spoke.

We stood in a long line that spilled out into the hall. It looked as if everybody took a noon lunch. Who was watching the patients, I wondered. After debating whether to try the special of the day, red snapper with overcooked vegetables, or to go for a sandwich, we settled on sandwiches and salad. Juggling our trays, we made our way through white and green-coated hospital personnel and visitors to a corner table.

Between bites of her ham sandwich , Julia said, "Thanks for being here when I needed a friend. Ugh," she muttered after taking a sip of her tepid coffee. Putting the cup down, she added, "Joe's boss, Frank Allen, tries to be comforting; but he's all business."

"And not very tactful. The other day we literally bumped into one another at a fire, and his words of greeting were, 'I might have known you'd be snooping around here.'"

"That's Frank, all right, but he is still a wonderful boss and a true friend to Joe." Her voice trailed off, and she began to sob. "I could have lost him in the accident and again today here in the hospital. Why?"

When she stopped to wipe her eyes and blow her nose, I asked what had happened to Joe this morning.

"Some time before the shift change at seven someone slipped into Joe's room and substituted another solution for his prescribed IV."

As she described this violation, she began to shake. I touched her arm and tried to calm her.

"I'll be all right," she said, brushing my hand aside. "It was awful. A few minutes after seven the day nurse came in to take Joe's blood pressure and had trouble getting a reading. After calling a doctor she checked the IV and spotted the change. She ran to the supply room and got the prescribed dosage Joe. Suspicious of the substitution, she saved the bag she'd found hanging from the stand after she had reconnected Joe to the right medication."

Julia started to cry again. Wiping her eyes, she continued. "By the time the doctor got there, Joe was almost gone. Dr. Long rushed into the room and slapped an oxygen mask on Joe and gave him a shot of adrenalin. He was removing the mask when you came into the room."

"But nobody except the hospital personnel and the law enforcement people knew where Joe was," I said.

"Somebody else did. And tried to kill my Joe."

While we were talking, I looked up and saw Frank Allen coming toward our table. Pulling up a chair and sitting down, he turned to Julia and said, "It was poison, just as the sheriff suspected. Another half hour and Joe would have been dead." Nodding a greeting to me, he said, "Glad you could come up here, Kay. Julia needs to get away from this nightmare for a little while." Looking around, he asked, "Where's Ted?"

"Back at the house. And I hope napping after our rough night over at the Abe Curtis place. You put us through a lot of crawling for clues. Turn up anything?"

"Might have. Can't say." Seeing the disgusted look on my face, Frank added, "You and Ted are very good crawlers. Do you do it often? Keeps you nimble, you know." Seeing me glance at my watch, he said, "Waiting for someone?"

"Yes, my son, Lew, and his family. They hope to take Lew's wife, Lora, home from the hospital today and expect to meet me in about five more minutes."

"How about hitching a ride back to your place with Julia and me?" Frank asked.

Julia started to protest. "I can't leave Joe."

"Nonsense. Joe doesn't need a sniffling wife around, while he is regaining his strength," Frank said.

"Boy, you are all tact," I said to Frank. Turning to Julia, I added, "Of course Ted and I would like you to stay with us. You can lie in the sun which promises to remain bright all afternoon. Or you can help me look for sand dollars down in our cove. The tide should be out in another hour."

I pushed back my chair and got up. "I'll tell my son about the change in plans. I'll be right back."

Lew was pulling into the parking lot as I walked down the hospital steps and Lora was with him. She leaned out to kiss me when I reached the car. I was pleased to see that Lew had tucked a blanket around her and that she was wearing a warm sweater. She still looked pale from her ordeal, but there was that familiar sparkle in her eyes. She would soon be in charge again.

Will and Tom clamored for attention in the back seat. "Grandma, you should have come on the Ferris wheel with us. Real scary!" Tom said.

"And I rode a giraffe instead of a horse on the merry-go-round," Will said, pushing his brother aside to lean out the window.

Hushing the boys, Lew said, "Hop in, Ms. Sleuth."

"Nope. I got a better offer. A ride back with Mr. Charm, Frank Allen."

When they looked puzzled, I explained that Frank was bringing both Julia Gilliam and me to our place. She needs a place to rest and a change from that hospital environment." When Lew started to ask about Joe, I said, "It's a long story. I'll tell you all about it, when I get home." Giving the boys a hug, I added, "Tell Grandpa to take another chicken out of the freezer for dinner."

Soon after Lew drove away, Frank Allen and Julia Gilliam came out the hospital door and headed toward a parked car. I hurried to join them.

On the ride to our place Frank relayed what little information he and the F.B.I. had on the persons they believed broke into Joe Gilliam's room. "One of those men you saw the other day, Kay. He dropped his tube of ointment on the ground outside Joe's window. Now we have to find him and his buddy."

When Frank swerved to miss a bicyclist and corrected the car a second before an oncoming vehicle zoomed by us, I closed my eyes and hoped we'd make it home unscathed. Closing my eyes was a mistake. I fell sound asleep. I woke with a start when Frank roused Julia and me in our driveway.

"Aren't you going to invite your chauffeur in for a cold drink?" he asked, getting out of the car and stretching. Seeing Ted walk over to greet us, Frank said to him, "Good thing somebody stayed awake on the drive from the hospital. These two insulted me by falling asleep right in the middle of a story I was telling."

"Come in and tell it to me, Frank. I'll listen," Ted said, as he helped me out of the back seat of the car. Looking at Julia, who had stepped out of the front seat, he said, "You must be Mrs. Gilliam. I'm Ted Roberts, Kay's better half."

"Don't brag," I said and kissed him. "And she's Julia to us." Glancing over his shoulder and bracing myself for the expected assault by the youngsters, I asked, "Where are the others?"

"Down in the cove. All except Lora, who's tucked in bed." Taking Julia's overnight bag, Ted added, "Wait until you see Eddie at work.

He's out in our rubber raft right now photographing our cove from the sea."

"So he's started his assignment. Have you been working with him?"I asked, handing him Julia's bag.

"I start tomorrow. Today he showed me how to make a good hitch on a tree or a sturdy bush and how to let him down a steep embankment. I'll demonstrate for you," he said, carrying Julia's bag to the porch and coming back with a large coil of rope. In less than a minute he held up the completed knot for our inspection. Basking in our praise at his accomplishment, he continued talking. "I'll practice pulling Eddie to safety first thing tomorrow on some small rise of land." Giving me a wry smile, he added, "It sure beats lecturing in front of a class."

"Just be careful and don't overdo," I warned.

"Stop fussing. I'll be all right," Ted said as we walked into the house. "I'll get us cold drinks," he added and darted into the kitchen.

As she stepped over the threshold Julia exclaimed, "What a pleasant living room you have! And windows that let you nestle in the shade of trees over here and enjoy glimpses of the ocean on this side. I hope the fog holds off so I can stand here and watch one of your famous sunsets today," she added before coming away from the windows and sinking into one of our comfortable, well worn chairs.

I was basking in her praise when Ted came from the kitchen carrying a tray with filled iced tea glasses. Looking around he asked, "Where's Frank?"

"I thought he was out in the kitchen with you," I said, going to the window. When I looked out, I saw Frank crawling on his knees in my flower garden. "What's he doing there? Ruining my nasturtiums? Now he's into the vegetable garden. Look at him finger the dirt, then lift the tomatoes on our plants."

"Maybe he's hungry," Ted said, as he nudged me aside and watched Frank. "I'll find out what he's hunting," he added, putting down the tray and going out to join Frank.

While we were waiting for the men to return, I told Julia we would put her on the sofa bed in the living room. "Not much privacy, but it's fairly comfortable. Oh, and you'll get to hear our mountain jays quarreling in that tree in the morning," I said, pointing to a large oak. "I'll change the sheets now," I added, bending over and pulling the sofa open.

"Let me help," Julia said, getting out of her chair. "Where do you keep the sheets?"

"In the cupboard in the hall. Thanks,"

I smiled at Julia when she returned lugging a blanket as well as sheets, a pillow case and a pillow tucked under her arm. "You remembered everything." Fitting a bottom sheet on the fold out bed, I said, "Our son, Eddie, slept here last night, but I'll put him in a sleeping bag in the grandsons' room. Will and Tom will like having their Uncle Eddie with them."

We were closing up the sofa bed, when Ted and Frank walked back in the house.

"What were you doing out there?" I asked Frank.

"What else? Snooping," he answered.

"Why?"

Grinning, Frank said, "Remember, I told you I ask the questions, not you."

Before I could retort, Ted handed us our glasses of tea and said, "Let's have our drinks and go down to the cove before the tide comes in." Turning to Julia, he said, "I see you're wearing good walking shoes. You'll need them when you make your way to the beach and over the slippery rocks down there."

A few minutes later we were slowly descending the side of the cliff. Julia stepped cautiously from one rise to the next and balanced herself with the trail side shrubs until they disappeared. A couple of times she got down on her knees and clutched one step while feeling with a free foot for the next lower tread. At last she reached the bottom and threaded her way among the rocks with us over to the water's edge. The tide was already starting to come in and was covering my favorite tide pool.

When I looked up after checking my footing, I saw Eddie paddling the raft toward us. When he reached shallow water, he climbed out. Making sure that his camera was securely sealed in its water-proof cover, he left it in the raft which he began guiding to shore.

Lew, who had come down to the beach earlier with his sons to play in the fast disappearing tide pools, stood up and walked over to help Eddie. "Here, I'll carry the raft for you. Grab your camera, and I'll hoist the boat over my shoulder."

"Thanks," Eddie said, and reached for his camera. The two of them were almost knocked over by an incoming wave as they waded to shore.

Glancing at Will and Tom, I saw they were scrambling to meet their dad and Uncle Eddie. "Stay back," I yelled, moving as quickly as possible over toward the boys.

Frank Allen was quicker than I. He grabbed the children's hands and held them firmly until Lew and Eddie were safely ashore. Then, releasing his grip on the boys, he led them to drier ground and sank down on a piece of driftwood. "You have to show a lot of respect for the sea, guys," he said, as I approached. "When it's time for the tide to come in, it pays no attention to us. It just keeps right on coming onto shore, and we have to get out of its way."

I could have hugged Frank for both protecting Will and Tom and for his gentle reminder of the power of the ocean. However, I resisted the impulse, for his next words were as rude as usual. "And what did you think you were doing, Kay? Trying to race across those slippery rocks!"

"Same as you, Frank, hoping to save the boys." Looking toward the cliff stairs, I saw Julia clutching one of the risers and starting to climb. "Come sit with us, Julia," I called out. "We'll be safe here for a little while."

When she still clung to the step I went to her and helped her walk over to the rest of our party lounging against the protected rocks. Seating her in a partially protected niche I said, "There's nothing like being close to the sea, hearing its murmur, then its roar, as fingers of water creep up the beach. Soon a tentative wave slithers close, then recedes. As long as we keep our eyes on the water's inward movement, we'll know when to leave the cove and climb back up the cliff."

In spite of my poetic description, I saw Julia shiver. Settling in her niche she looked to the sea and began to relax when Lew and Eddie joined us.

When water started splashing closer to Ted on a big rock jutting into the sea he climbed down and joined us.

For the next several minutes all of us were silent as we watched the pulsating sea. Will and Tom curled up in their dad's arms. Even Julie seemed to lose her fear of the ocean as we sat there. When one large wave moved rapidly up the beach and sprayed us with salt water, we got up and walked to the foot of the stairs to begin our climb home.

Frank declined our invitation to stay for dinner. "See you in the morning," he said to Julia. "And don't worry about Joe. We have guards all around the hospital."

I waved to Frank before stepping into the house to start dinner. Lora had beaten me to it. She was shelling peas as I walked into the kitchen.

Looking up at me, she said, "I can make us a chicken

casserole for supper, if you wish." Before I could answer, she added, "I found a cooked chicken breast in your freezer and can zap it in the microwave oven for a few minutes. All right?"

"Perfect," I said, and added, "It's wonderful to see you taking charge again." I paused before saying, "I remember the first time I met you. You were directing a play at the college and seemed to have everything and everybody under control."

"You mean I was bossy," she said, and grinned.

"No, just completely on top of things. And with a touch of direction that was needed that day."

"What a subtle way of describing me. Thanks, Mom. Now, if you would rather take over the dinner, I'll graciously bow out of the kitchen."

"And leave me stranded? A chicken casserole will be fine. I'll put together a salad." Studying her still wan face, I added, "You are either making a fast recovery, or you are putting on a great act."

"A little of both. I still feel weak and blue, but there's no sense in fretting over our loss." Cocking her head to one side, she asked, " How would you like to have another grandchild within the year?"

"That soon?"

"Why not? Dr. Long suggests it, and who am I to go against the worthy doctor?"

"Good luck!" I said and gave her a hug.

While I chopped lettuce for the salad, I asked, "Did you see Frank Allen leave?"

"No. I didn't know he was here," she answered, stooping over to pick up a pea pod that had escaped her pile.

I walked over and looked out the window. "What's Frank doing this time?" I asked watching him crawl around outside our bedroom.

When he saw me, he grinned but kept on searching the ground. Soon he got to his feet; dusted the dirt off his knees and hands and headed toward the front of the house. He didn't come in but climbed into his car and drove off.

Just as well. He wouldn't have told me anything if I'd asked. He would remind me that he asked the questions, not I.

While we ate dinner, we listened to the news. "The fire department and the sheriff's office have found that the fire was deliberately set at the Curtis place last night. No suspects have been brought in for questioning."

There was no word on the attempted murder of Joe Gilliam.

We were finishing dessert when the telephone rang. When I answered, the caller asked to speak to Mrs. Joe Gilliam. "This is the hospital calling," the voice said.

"For you, Julia. It's the hospital."

Julia grabbed the phone from me and said, "Mrs. Gilliam speaking."

She listened, then cried out, "Oh, no!"

CHAPTER NINE

Julia's hand shook as she clutched the phone and the words of the caller reached our ears. 'Mr. Gilliam has had a relapse. Come immediately."

"Not again," Julia cried into the line that had gone dead. Turning an ashen face to us, she said, "Somebody loan me your car, please. I have to get up to the hospital right away. Oh, God!"

"We'll take you, Julia,"Ted said. "You may have to spend the night, so throw a few things in your bag; and we'll leave now."

"Not so fast,"I said, going over and holding the shaking Julia in my arms. "This may be a hoax. Who called? It wasn't Dr. Long's voice or the nurse, Annabelle. I've heard that voice before but not at the attendance desk or in Joe's room."

"So what? Someone from the hospital called, and we have to get Julia up there right away,"Ted said.

"Something feels wrong,"I argued. Let me call Frank Allen." While Ted was ignoring me and looking for the car keys, I felt around in the flower pot where I'd put Frank's telephone number.

While I listened to the ringing, Ted grabbed my arm and said, "Are you crazy? Come on."

Julia was slipping on her jacket and heading for the door when someone came on the line.

Brushing Ted's hand away, I said, "Let me speak to Frank Allen. Yes, this is an emergency. My name? Kay Roberts."

There were murmurs on the other end of the line. Then I heard that familiar voice. "Agent Allen speaking. What is it, Kay?"

When I told him about the call, supposedly from the hospital, he barked, "Hang up, but stay by the phone. Don't let anyone leave the house."

When he slammed the phone in my ear, I told the others what Allen had said. In less than five minutes Frank was back on the line.

"Nothing's the matter with Joe. One of our men is sitting by his bedside. Another is just outside his door, and another is patrolling the grounds. Stay put. I'll be right over."

While we waited for Frank, Julia kept asking, "Is Joe really all right? Who would play such a dirty trick on us? Who, besides you folks and Frank know I am here?"

No one spoke. Even Will and Tom were frightened into silence. Noone here could answer her questions. Half an hour later we heard a car turn into our driveway and hurried out to the porch to meet Frank.

Although wisps of fog were moving shore ward, there was still enough light for Frank to check around outside our house again.

Turning to Eddie, Frank said, "Bring your camera. I want to get a shot of this spot under the window."

What spot, I wondered, and shivered at the thought of someone spying right outside our window.

Satisfied that he could do nothing more outside, Frank followed us into the house and plunked down on the couch. Before he could catch his breath and speak, Julia said, "I want to talk with Joe. No, not later, Frank, right now."

"Calm down, Julia. Joe may be asleep. Maybe he's been given a sleeping pill."

"Well, wake him up. I want to talk to him now,"she cried. Handing Frank the phone, she ordered him to phone the hospital.

Shrugging his shoulders, he did as she asked. After assuring the receptionist that Mrs. Gilliam had to speak to her husband, we heard a groggy voice slur a hello and mumble "Fine Julia. Let me sleep."

There was silence for a few seconds before we heard the phone clatter to the floor.

Satisfied that her husband was really there and alive, Julia put down our phone and smiled at us. "He's going to be all right, I know."

Turning to Frank, she thanked him for indulging her need to talk with Joe.

"Some conversation you had,"Frank said, and grinned at her. Settling back on the couch, he continued, "Thank God, someone had the good sense to phone me. You would probably have been ambushed on the road to the hospital tonight." Looking at me, he added, "It had to be you. You're the only one who has my telephone number."

When I nodded, he asked, "Want to join the force?"

"No way,"I answered.

Ted interrupted this exchange, saying "Kay got suspicious about the caller. Thought she recognized the man's voice."

Julia spoke up. "Who knows I'm here? And why would he try to scare me into driving up to the hospital?"

"Someone knows you're here. While you and Kay slept on the trip back from Point Arno today, I spotted a dark blue sedan tailing us. Why would anyone want to scare you into going up there tonight, you ask? To kidnap you. Joe may have said something to you that at the moment means nothing to you. Those out to get Joe probably hope to squeeze that information out of you."

While we were talking, Will and Tom ran outside to play in the fading light. We were so absorbed in our conversation, that we didn't miss them until they burst in the house and ran to their dad.

"Someone's out there,"they whispered.

Lora held out her arms to Tom, who climbed in her lap and started to cry.

Will, perched on his father's lap, said, "We were playing hide and seek when Tom saw something move behind that big tree by the bedroom window. He thought it was me and was sneaking up to catch me, when a man stepped out and walked toward the road."

"I was so scared,"Tom said. "I yelled to Will, 'Allee-allee ox in free,' and he jumped out of the bushes near me."

"I was scared too. I saw the man walk toward the road,"Will said.

While the boys were telling their story, Frank had disappeared. A few minutes later he returned to say that he spotted a car parked down the road turn on its lights and drive away. "It was too dark to make out the model or its color." Without asking, Frank went to the phone and dialed. "Allen here. Send a surveillance backup out here now.

You know where I am."

"But he's driven away, so we're safe,"Julia said.

"As the wife of one of our agents, you know better than that. You're to be guarded as carefully as Joe." Giving us an exasperated look, he added, "And now we have to protect this family as well."

"Thank you for your gracious concern for us,"I said.

"Always delighted to serve you, ma'am,"Frank answered and bowed.

It wasn't long before we heard a faint whistle outside and saw Frank relax. "You'll be all right now,"he said, getting to his feet and going toward the door. "See you in the morning,"he called over his shoulder as he descended the porch steps.

"How did he know someone from his office had come here?" I asked.

"We'll never know. We'll just have to hope we're safe for the night," Ted said.

CHAPTER TEN

"Hey, it's not even nine o'clock. Seems as if it's been hours since that fake hospital call. Who's ready for a fast game of cribbage?" Ted said, locking the door and peering out the living room window. "I'm getting as edgy as an old woman,"he added and grinned.

"Sexist remark,"I retorted. "You can do better than that."

"No bickering, you two,"Eddie said. "I'll take you on, Dad, and beat the socks off you. Where's the cribbage board?"

While Eddie and Ted were setting up the cribbage board and putting the pegs in place, Lew and Lora tucked their young ones into bed. Julia, who slumped on the couch, was almost asleep. I whispered to Ted and Eddie to move their game into the kitchen then gently touched Julia on the shoulder and suggested she turn in for the night.

"Bathroom's free. While you're in there, I'll pull out your bed,"I told her.

"Thanks. I am exhausted. Think Joe's asleep?"

"Let's hope so,"I said and sent her on her way to the bathroom.

When Julia was settled for the night, I went out on the porch to listen to the lapping of the waves and feel the fog dampen my cheeks. I was almost asleep when Lew and Lora come to join me.

"Mom, we're staying until we know you and Dad are safe,"Lew said.

When I started to protest, Lora added, "No arguments, Mom. So, old Ben Franklin said that guests, like fish, should be gone by the fourth day. We're not guests, but family. You're stuck with us until this situation is cleared up."

"Of course I love having you with us, but we can take care of ourselves. Besides, no one is bothering Dad or me. And what about your job, Lew? You can't just walk away from it."

"Watch me. I'll phone tomorrow and get family leave. Then we're going to get to the bottom of this mystery. " Shifting in his chair, he continued. "Who is snooping around here, leaving footprints under your bedroom window?"

Maybe Will or Tom, when they played hide and seek."

"You know better than that. And why is someone out to get that F.B.I. agent, Joe Gilliam? They got his partner, all right. And that man who was shot in the back. Who was he? And what about that arson fire at your neighbor's place?

Lora interrupted Lew and said, "What is there is this quiet place that attracts criminal activity?"

"Promise you won't laugh at my idea?"I asked.

"Not a snicker. Shoot."

"I believe someone wants to build a reactor to extract hydrogen from sea water near us,"I said.

"What for? And how did you get this crazy idea?"

"You promised not to laugh,"I reminded him.

"I'm not laughing. I'm stunned. What would someone do with the hydrogen?"

"Listen to this. Just the day before you arrived, Dad read the weirdest story in the newspaper to me. I remember; I was jogging in place and almost fell off the trampoline."

"Go on. What was the story?"

"Scientists from the United States, Japan and Russia have proposed a permanent manned lunar station to mine moon rocks for helium-3 to fuse with hydrogen from sea water to produce a cheap and safe form of energy."

"Boy, that's a mouthful; but what has it to do with you?"Lew said.

Lora was sitting on the edge of her chair and leaning toward me. "How do the scientists propose to get those rocks from the moon? And, if and when they do, where will they store them? And how and where on this earth would scientists extract the hydrogen?" Lora gave a little gasp. "Mom, you're thinking about the location of the reactor that would be needed for this extraction and fusion, aren't you? How exciting!"

"Wait a minute. You two are way ahead of me, Lew said. "Such a reactor could be anywhere on the globe that touches an ocean."

"Not just any place. It would need to be an isolated location, away from port cities with their pollution,"I said.

"But it should be a flat beach area,"Lora said, getting into the spirit of our speculations.

"That lets this coast out of the running,"Lew said.

"Not necessarily. How about that piece of property just north of the folks—Abe Curtis' place?"

Lew and I were silent as we remembered that awful night of the fire at the Curtis'. Could there be a connection to this possible search for flat beach land and the arson?

I shook my head, trying to stop this wild guessing. One newspaper article shouldn't set us to thinking about such a possibility. On the other hand, why had Eddie's company sent him up here to photograph in detail the fifteen miles of ocean front which included our lot and the one owned by Abe Curtis? Eddie hadn't told us whether this was a Federal government contract, one from aninternational conglomerate, or a local real estate group. I decided not to share these thoughts with Lora and Lew. It would make them worry even more about Ted and me.

While we were talking, Ted came out and put his hands on my shoulders. "Time for bed, Kay. Eddie's already climbed into his sleeping bag in the boys' room." Helping me to my feet, he said to Lora, "I don't know about these two who spent most of last night at the Curtis fire, but I'm bushed. Glad you didn't have to live through that nightmare."

"Lora had her own nightmare,"I said to Ted.

"Sorry, Lora. I wasn't thinking."

Lora reached up and kissed Ted good night and said, "I understand, Dad. It's something I want to forget, too, as soon as possible."

Before long the house was quiet except for an occasional snore from Ted and from someone in the boys' room. I drifted off to sleep in Ted's arms.

I jerked awake the next morning when Ted dropped one of his shoes. Sitting up in bed and rubbing my eyes, I saw him bend down near the door to retrieve the shoe, and give me a sheepish grin.

"Sorry about that, Kay. I meant to tiptoe out of here and let you sleep."

"Six o'clock!"I said, glancing at the bedside clock. "What got you up so early?"

"Big job this morning. Eddie wants to put me through a quick training course on how to rope him when he gets down into one of those steep ravines near the house."

Stifling the urge to discourage his taking this risk, I went over and put my arms around him. "Just be careful, Ted."

"That's no fun,"he said, and pinched my bottom.

When we walked into the kitchen, Eddie was fussing with the coffee maker. Julia, who was putting the sofa bed back together for day use, said, "Let me fix breakfast for you early birds. Then Kay and I can have a leisurely breakfast while you wrestle with ropes and cameras."

"Great! I'll dash into the bathroom and be gorgeous in a few minutes,"I said. As I climbed out of the shower, I heard low voices outside the window. Clutching my towel, I sidled over to the window and caught the end of a conversation.

"Better keep an eye on the ravine behind you,"a man said. "One of them may still be down there."

Who might still be down there? What had our guards seen? I shuddered at the thought of an intruder. Maybe Lew and Lora were right. We needed their protection as well as Frank Allen's and his crew. Shoving these frightening thoughts aside, I dressed and joined the others at breakfast.

CHAPTER ELEVEN

I was too late to eat with Ted and Eddie. They were already strapping equipment on Eddie. While they tussled with the gear, Eddie gave instruction to Ted on how to handle the rope. Glancing down, I saw that Eddie was wearing shoes that looked strong enough to hold a mountain climber.

"Where do you going to start?"I asked.

"Straight down from your house, Mom. Want to watch?"

"Promise you won't fall?"

"Boy, what a lot of faith you have in us!" Eddie said and added, "I'll yell to you, when I think I'm about to plunge to my death."

"Do that, and I'll take your picture for the newspaper,"I retorted, pulling his hair.

When Julia and I took our coffee cups and followed Ted, we saw Eddie inching his way down the side of the ravine. He stopped at intervals and checked his camera. Once he focused on a spot and snapped a picture.

"Just checking," he called up to us. "No need to take my picture yet, Mom."

When his feet touched the beach, Eddie signaled to Ted to throw him one end of the rope. I found I was clutching my cup so tightly I feared I might crack it. "Relax, Kay," I muttered to myself. "Ted knows what he's doing." As I watched, Ted twirled the rope and dropped one end right into Eddie's hand. "Good shot!" I

74

whispered to Julia.

As we stood rooted to the edge of the cliff, we saw Eddie encircle his waist with the rope and pull on it. Ted began reeling in the line. Soon Eddie's feet were dangling in space. Next Eddie was balancing on an outcropping of earth and rock and then toeing his way out of the canyon toward Ted.

I felt weak with relief. But it wasn't over yet. The men practiced the routine for the next hour. Every so often Eddie stopped to photograph an area while swaying at the end of the rope. Finally satisfied with the morning's routine, he signaled to Ted to bring him up to safety. I could see Ted struggle with the rope, but in spite of the strain, he looked happy.

While we stood there stiff from the tension of watching these dangerous maneuvers, Lew came up behind us. "Good show?" he asked, bringing Will and Tom over to us. "How are they doing?"

"Best show in town. Look at Eddie swinging out in space. Oh, good, he's on firm ground again." Pointing up the hill, I said, "Look at your dad and granddad pull on the rope."

Will and Tom were jumping up and down beside us and yelling, "Can we do that, Dad?"

"Maybe when you're older. Come on. Let's go back in the house and try those doughnuts you talked me into buying at the bakery in town."

"Mmm, doughnuts!   Enough for all of us?" I asked, following Lew and the boys. Julia lingered a few minutes to watch Eddie stop for one more shot of terrain before signaling to be pulled to safety. Soon I heard her running to catch up with us.

"Plenty of doughnuts for everybody, including our runner, Julia," Lew said, as we stopped to wait for her. "Also enough for another hungry person, my sleepy wife."

"What sleepy wife?" Lora asked, coming out the door with a white paper bag in her hand. "Terrible room service around here. I had to find my own cold cereal," she added, giving Lew a kiss. "What's all the ruckus out here?"

"First day of the camera crew in action," Lew explained.

"Dad's doing a great job and loving it. Eddie's in his element. Want to take a peek?"

"Sure, as soon as I dig out a doughnut to hold me until lunch time," she said, reaching into the sack and pulling out a chocolate covered one. Want one?" she asked, handing the sack to Will.

Will seized the bag and retrieved a jelly-filled pastry before handing the sack to his brother and running to catch up with his parents on their walk to the edge of the cliff.

Julia and I jumped and almost dropped our coffee cups we were refilling, when a voice, just outside the kitchen window said, "Got any food for a starving F.B.I. crew?"

I turned to the window and stared into the face of Frank Allen.

"Are you going to stand there or let us in?"

"Sure. Come on in," I said, unlocking the back door and waiting for the three men. They were covered with vines and wore soiled brown cotton work gloves.

Seeing me stare at their appearance, Frank said, "What did you expect an agent to wear? A tux?" Nodding toward one of the men, who had a spider making its way along the vine in his hair, "Warren's been crawling over every inch of your land. Says you could do with some cleanup around here."

Ignoring Frank's rudeness, I said to Warren, "Nice spider you're wearing. A black widow?"

"I hope not. I'll check it out , when I wash my hands. Do you mind if I use your bathroom?"

"Of course not. Show him where it is, Frank."

It felt good to give Frank an order.

When the two men disappeared down the hall, I turned to the other agent - Homer, Frank had said - and asked, "How do you like your eggs, scrambled or fried?"

"Any way except raw, ma'am. I'm starved," he said, taking my hint and washing his hands in the kitchen sink

While Frank and his two agents scarfed down bacon, eggs and toast, Frank told Julia and me that there had been poachers in our cove this morning. Clothed in a wet suit, one man was searching among the rocks. When he spotted Homer, watching him, he scuttled back in the water and waded out to a raft bobbing in the waves and holding a second person.

"Maybe he was looking for the surveyor's compass," I said.

"Could be," Frank said, wiping egg and toast crumbs from his chin. Turning to Julia, he asked, "Want me to drive you up to visit Joe this morning?"

"Yes. When?"

"Right now," Frank said, and added to his two-man crew, "Your relief should be here in another hour. You know where to reach me." As he started out the front door, Frank asked whether Ted and I planned to visit Joe today.

"Yes, as soon as Ted's rested from his morning's workout on the cliff, we'll drive up to Point Arno. Why do you suppose he wants to see us?" I asked. "Think he's up to a visit from us?"

"I heard he's giving the hospital staff fits, because he wants to get out of there and catch the devil who got his partner and tried to do him in."

"Doesn't he know that one devil is dead with a bullet in his back?"

"With what he's gone through, he probably doesn't know about that murder," Frank said, before taking Julia's arm and steering her down the steps toward his car.

As soon as the other agents finished their meal, they thanked me and disappeared into the brush somewhere outside. I might not hear their relief give a whistle, when he or she arrived. Talk about secretive!

Soon after Frank and Julia left, Ted and Eddie came dragging themselves and their equipment into the house. Will and Tom danced around them, buffeting them with questions. Was it fun swinging out in space? Was it hard pulling Uncle Eddie up the side of the cliff? When could they try?

"Not for a long time, boys," Eddie rumpled Will's hair. "Want to see pictures of camels? And I got a good picture of a pyramid, when I was in Egypt."

"Sure. What's a pyramid?" Tom asked.

"You'll see," Eddie answered, taking the youngsters with him into their shared room.

Lew and Lora strolled into the house bringing the mail and the newspaper. "We knew the hard-working roper wouldn't have time for his daily trek to the post office, so we did it for him," Lew said, and began sorting the mail. "Something for Eddie, and here's that new book you wanted, Dad. Still working on the local Indians?"

Ted nodded and reached for the package. "Hope this one has what I need," he said, tearing off the wrapping and starting to examine the book.

After Ted took a short nap, he and I started for Point Arno. As I pulled onto the highway, Ted put on a tape of soft music and said, "Wow, our first time out alone since the grandkids came a month ago! What can we do to celebrate?"

"How about a rich chocolate sundae after our visit with Joe Gilliam? No, you prefer strawberry."

"Or we could skip the ice cream and have dinner up there. Any good place to eat?"

"There's a fish place a few miles beyond Point Arno. It's supposed to be special." Glancing out to sea, I pointed and said, "Look at the boats coming in with their daily catch. Hope they were all lucky."

We were so involved in planning our free time that we didn't, at first, notice the dark blue car behind us. Just as I passed a van and slipped back into my lane, I saw the blue car speed up and zoom past the van, barely missing an on-coming truck. The blue car almost ran into us, as its driver squeezed in behind us.

"What's that fool doing?" I asked Ted, who was sitting on the edge of his seat, straining at his seat belt.

By now the driver of the blue car had slowed down, seemingly to keep pace with us. When I peered in my rear view mirror, I saw there were two men in the car.

"I'm going to pull into the gas station up the road about a mile. We need to fill up, and it will get that jerk off our tail."

"Good idea. You don't suppose Frank has someone following us, do you?"

"If so, I hope he learns to drive. Oh, there's the station. Got your credit card?"

"Yes," Ted said, fumbling in his jacket pocket and bringing out the card. "Oh, oh, they are stopping here, too. I'll fill the tank. You phone Frank Allen. Got his number?"

"Yes. In my head," I said, getting change out of my purse for the phone call. "Be careful, hon," I added.

"You, too, Kay," Ted said, walking with me into the station to leave his credit card.

One of the men from the blue car followed us into the place. When he saw me looking back at him, he smiled, displaying a chipped tooth. I suppressed a gasp and hurried to the phone at the back of the store. While Ted took care of the car, I dialed Frank's number and luckily reached him.

"Yes, Kay. What is it?"

"Trouble, I think. Ted and I are on the road to the hospital and being followed. Are they your agents?"

"No. Stay there at the gas station. About five miles south of the hospital, you say?"

"Yes," I whispered into the phone, when I saw Chapped Tooth looking at me.

Frank's voice came back on the line. "A helicopter will drop down there in about five minutes. Do what you're told to do," he said, and hung up on me.

As I walked away from the phone, I was shaking so hard I had to steady myself on the freezer before walking up front to the counter. Chipped Tooth was counting out change from his purchase of candy and gum. Yes, he was the same man who'd taunted his poison ivy partner at the hospital. No sense in trying to avoid him, just confront him.

"How is your friend? Poison ivy all cleared up?" I asked, putting on my best imitation smile.

"Thought I recognized you," he drawled. "My friend? He's better. What a pain in the ass he is."

I looked out the door and saw Ted signaling for me to hurry up. "In a minute, Ted. I'm getting a candy bar to stave off my hunger. Want one?"

Sensing something was happening, Ted said, "No. I'll skip the sweets, but hurry up. The fish won't wait."

"Fish in your car?" Chipped Tooth asked, giving me a suspicious look.

I had to think up something real quick. "No. We're heading for that super fish market up the road. Best red snapper around."

"Where's that?" the woman behind the counter asked.

Blast her! Stalling for time, I said, "You live around here and haven't heard of that market? Here, give me a piece of paper, and I'll write down the name of it for you. Oh, yes, it's in Point Arno. Want me to draw you a map?"

Fortunately she had to hunt for paper, and then she couldn't find a pencil or a map. Where was that helicopter?

"Here's a map. Just write the name on it, if you will. And here's a stub of a pencil. Good enough?"

"Swell," I muttered, and began searching for the non-existent fish market's street. Here was the longest street in town. I could feel Chipped Tooth nudging close to me and saw him watching my markings. However, I was saved from completing this lie by the sound of the helicopter overhead.

"Well, I never," the clerk exclaimed, as she came from behind the counter and went to the door to watch the helicopter land on the gravel pull-out of the station.

Expecting to see Frank step down from the copter, I was stunned to see a tiny woman jump down and run to Ted, standing beside our car.

Who in the world was she?

CHAPTER TWELVE

I stared as Ted gathered this small person in his arms. Still chattering, she walked with him toward me. When they were close, I yelled, "B.C!"and ran to her.

"Surprised, Kay?"she asked, when she reached up and kissed me.

"Stunned."

She cut my flow of questions short by whispering, "Get in the helicopter. Quick."

So Frank and the F.B.I. team had called in my old friend, B.C., to help with the investigation.

As I walked on shaky legs over to the helicopter, a man climbed down and greeted me. Offering me his hand, he said, "Hi, I'm Ricky. I'll drive your car, Mrs. Roberts, so you and your husband can catch up on news with B.C. on your ride into town." Watching me climb in, he said, "First time for you in one of these?"

"No, but I'll enjoy it. Thanks for rescuing us."

"Ricky made a detour on his way to our car and stopped to speak to the passenger in the dark blue car. As I waved good bye to Ricky, I got a good look at the passenger. He was the poison ivy patient, Whiny.

Chipped Took darted over to his car and said something to Ricky. Although I couldn't hear his words over the whir of the blades, his gestures and sneer were enough. Ricky must have told him a plausible story because Chipped Tooth laughed and got in his car and drove away.

While I was watching the action on the ground, B.C. radioed her office. "A OK,"she said and broke the connection. Settling back in her seat, she said, "First I meet you on the island off Santa Barbara. Now up here on the north coast. When did you move here?"

"As soon as we finished the assignment on the island. It should be opening soon as the newest national park. But you. What's the story with you?"I asked.

"Same old routine. Trying to keep the good guys like you two alive and catch the criminals." Giving us that jaunty grin I knew so well, she added, "It sure gives me an appetite. Want to take me for a snack after you talk with Joe?"

"Not a snack, but how about out to a restaurant for a fish dinner?" Ted said.

"Great! I'll munch on crackers until you're ready,"she said, reaching into her knapsack and bringing out cheese crackers. Wiping a cracker crumb off her chin, she pointed and said, "There's the hospital. I'll wait for Ricky in the parking lot."

"What's he going to do about those two men?"I asked.

"Sorry. Classified information,"she answered.

I shrugged my shoulders. No sense trying to get information out of her or her boss, Frank Allen. When I hopped out of the helicopter, I blew her a kiss and said we would only stay a short while with Joe.

"Then it's up the coast for dinner,"Ted said. "Don't eat too many of those,"he added, pointing at the almost empty package of crackers.

This time the nurse, Annabelle, recognized me and greeted me warmly. " He's been waiting to see both of you. Not too patiently,"she added and grinned as she took us down the hall to Joe Gilliam's room.

Joe was sitting up in a chair and holding Julia's hand. "Took you long enough to get here,"he said, shaking Ted's hand and smiling at me. "Any trouble?"

"A little,"Ted said. Not wanting to worry the Gilliams, he

changed the subject. Pulling up a chair beside Joe, he said, "Tell us what you remember about the accident, Mr. Gilliam."

"Cut the formalities. Call me Joe." Wincing as he shifted in his chair, he said, "What do I remember? The crash, of course, then nothing until I woke up here in the hospital. Frank's been trying to jog my memory." Shaking his head, he added, "How can I remember nothing? He keeps saying there may be something I know and maybe told Julia after I woke up." Joe jerked forward in his chair and spat out, "Did they think I'd put Julia in danger by blabbing information? All I'm certain of is that they whoever they were wanted to snuff out both Kent O'Brien and me to make sure we didn't get to talk to our F.B.I. boss."

"They? I understood only one man's been identified as ramming your panel truck. And he's dead. Were there two in the truck?"I asked.

"I don't know." A strange look crossed Joe's face.

"What is it, Joe?"Julia asked.

Ignoring her question, he said, "Did you find my fishing gear when you and Frank went to the Allison house?"

"No, and I thought it strange that you and Kent hadn't tried your hand at fishing up here,"Julia said.

Joe slammed his hand down on the arm of the chair. "The truck. It's in the truck."

"What's in the truck?"I asked

"Gosh, you're slow. What have I been talking about? The truck. My fishing gear,"he yelled.

Turning to Julia, I said, "He was just as rude the first time I saw him. Called me a snoopy woman."

Joe let out a belly laugh. "And salty, I remember." Leaning forward in his chair and lowering his voice, he said, "Get that fishing gear and give it to Frank. Tell him to come here with it, and I'll show him something that may be a clue. Something I found caught on seaweed when Kent and I were paddling back from the sea lions that day I met you, Kay."

Ted got up and said, "I'll call Frank from here. What's the number, Kay?" When I gave it to him, he left the room.

Although Joe looked exhausted from our visit, he was too excited to nap before he had a report from Frank. When I got up to leave, he said, "No, sit down and wait with Julia and me." Turning to her, he said, "Staying for supper with me?"

"Yes, if I can hitch a ride back to the Roberts' place."

"Of course. Ted and I are taking a friend on up the coast for a fish dinner and will swing back to get you." Giving Joe a sly grin, I added, "Besides this snoopy woman wants to know what Frank Allen finds."

Ted was gone a long time. When he returned, he said he had reached Frank who was going over immediately to the garage and check out the wrecked panel truck. "He told me to wait by the phone until he reported back that he had the gear. I thought the phone would never ring."

Slouching at the foot of the bed, Ted continued. "While I waited for Frank's call, a woman sauntered over to the phone and took her sweet time chatting with a friend on the line while I stewed. Finally she hung up, and Frank got through to me. He's on his way to the hospital."

When Ted finished his complaint about the talkative woman on the phone, he looked at his watch and stood up. "We'd better be on our way, Kay. Our friend will be gnawing on her notebook if we don't get her fed shortly."

Getting up and following Ted toward the door, I said to Julia, "We'll be back in a couple of hours to pick you up. Hope the fog holds off until we make it home."

B.C. was sitting on the hospital steps talking with the pilot., Ricky. When he saw us, he handed our car keys to Ted and said, "I'd better try to get back to headquarters before this fog socks us in. See you tomorrow, B.C."

"Sure thing,"B.C. said. "Thanks, Ricky."

"Ready for some real food, B.C.?"I asked as we climbed into our car.

"Always ready,"she answered as we drove out of the parking lot and onto the highway.

Over a marvelous salad and fresh-caught fish, we talked

about our time on the island and brought B.C. up to date on our mutual friends. When the dessert menu came, B.C. ordered pie ala mode. Where did she put all that food on her tiny frame?

The port and starboard lights on the boats heading into the harbor glowed in the early evening light. We watched as the last of the fishing boats glided in and berthed for the night. There were three pleasure boats moored at the dock. Sea gulls dived for fish while sea lions played around the boats. As we walked back to our car, we heard the fog horn tolling out beyond the breakwater.

Frank Allen and Julia were waiting on the hospital steps when we pulled into the parking lot. "I'll take B.C. back with me,"Frank said, helping Julia into the back seat of our car. ·

B.C. hopped out on the other side and came around to the front of the car to kiss me good night. "Thanks for dinner, you two. It was fun, wasn't it?"

"Yes, including the helicopter ride. Come out to our place if Frank will let you." Leaning out the window, I said to Frank, "Did you find any clue in the fishing gear?"

"No comment,"he said.

I rolled up the window, and we took off for home.

By the time we left the comforting lights of Point Arno, the fog was thick on the ground. Ted slowed to a crawl, and I leaned out my window to watch for deer on the road. We knew the ocean was only a few yards below us, but we couldn't even hear the sound of the surf or the warning from the fog horn off the point. Occasionally pinpoints of light penetrated the fog, as a northbound car approached us.

Julia, checking the back window, scooted forward and reported that a car had been following us ever since we left Point Arno.

"Not again,"I said and started to shake. However we must have passed a side road a mile or so further south, because that car signaled and turned left. What a relief! We now had the road to ourselves for a few miles until another car made its ghostly appearance from the south and vanished in the fog.

It was almost ten o'clock before we turned into our

driveway. Both Lew and Eddie came out to greet us as Ted parked in the car port.

"Are we ever glad to see you folks,"Eddie said. "They've just reported an accident north of here. A head-on collision."

Before we could speak, we heard the wail of a siren.

The highway patrol must be on its way, or maybe that was the ambulance,"I said. "What a night to be out on the road!"

Lora took one look at our weary faces and headed for the kitchen. In a few minutes she met us in the living room with cups of tea for all of us.

"Plasma,"I murmured, along with my thanks, and sipped the hot brew.

Ted, who had made a quick stop in the bathroom, returned and asked Julia what Frank Allen had reported on his find of the fishing gear.

"He sure was close-mouthed with us,"I said.

"That's Frank, all right,"Julia said. "He sent me out of the room when he came in lugging the fishing gear. Said he didn't want to get me involved."

"Typical,"I muttered.

"And sensible. The less Julia knows, the safer she is,"Ted reminded me. Glancing at the living room clock, he added, ""Let's catch the late news. There may be something about the accident."

After listening to the usual commercials, the newscaster came on and said, "The highway patrol has just reported they have found a dark blue car abandoned in a ditch off the highway near Point Arno. The engine was still warm. There was no identification on the vehicle. The only articles found were a candy wrapper and a half-empty tube of poison ivy medication.."

Poison ivy medication? Candy wrapper? Chills went up and down my spine. Could Chipped Tooth and his pal, Whiny, be the victims?

CHAPTER THIRTEEN

Trying not to visualize an open-mouthed Chipped Tooth and a poison ivy speckled man lying somewhere near the abandoned car, I listened to Eddie map out plans for tomorrow. "We'll start on that property next to yours on the north side, Dad, and move on up the coast." Stopping to take a sip of his replenished tea, he added, "I got a letter from my boss today. He's getting antsy. Wants me to speed up my survey. 'What's taking you so long?' he complained." Giving us a mischievous grin, Eddie said, "Gotta please the man. After all, he's my bread and butter."

"What a difference in bosses,"Lew said. When I called about taking family leave, Jack asked what the trouble was and then sent this best to the folks. He even urged me to take as much as two weeks off. It's a slack time at the office, he reminded me."

"If I get fired, I can move in with you and Lora and the boys. I need a good cook, Lora,"Eddie said.

"And wash your socks? Forget it,"Lora retorted, giving Eddie a hug.

"What a family!"Ted said. "But let's get back to business. What do you plan to do on you leave, Lew?"

"First thing tomorrow I want to go to the county court house over in Ukiah and look up the deeds for the property around here. See whether any lots have recently changed hands." Turning to Lora, he said, "You and the boys can roam around the town. Find a good picnic spot for lunch.

Play catch or feed the ducks in the pond while I go through those old dusty files at the court house."

As we were preparing for bed, I heard the now familiar whistle. This must be the changing of the guards outside. B.C. might be one of them tonight. Maybe she would come in covered with ivy and wearing dirty work gloves tomorrow and have breakfast with us.

"I hope she doesn't stick her face in poison ivy out there,"I muttered under my breath. Hoisting myself up from the couch, I said to Julia, "It's all yours. Sweet dreams."

Usually Ted is snoring before I fall asleep, but tonight he was still sorting his gear for tomorrow when I drifted off to sleep. I awoke to the mournful sound of the fog horn. "When I drew back the curtain, I looked into a blanket of fog.

I was still standing at the window, when I heard the scraping of feet on the porch and the high-pitched voices of Will and Tom. I hoped they and their dad hadn't tried to go down to the cove on those wet steps. I reached for my robe and headed for the shower. When I walked into the kitchen after dressing, Ted, Eddie and the boys were finishing breakfast.

"Good morning, sleeping beauty,"Ted said. I always feel ten years younger when Ted says that.

"Hi, Grandma. Want some cereal?"Will asked, holding up a box of Wheaties.

"Sure do, but first I want to see whether my friend, B.C., is outside,"I said, going to the door and looking out. "No one there,"I reported, closing the door and coming back to the table. It was then that I heard a rustle outside the kitchen window.

A bunch of leaves appeared with a familiar face peeking out of them. "Some bird dog you'd make,"B.C. said, brushing a couple of long stems out of her eyes. "What's for breakfast?"

"Come in and help yourself,"I said as I heard the whistle. The next shift had arrived.

While B.C. gorged herself at the breakfast table, we watched the fog begin to dissipate and the sun gain strength. Eddie and Ted picked up their equipment and left the house. After gulping a cup of coffee and packing a picnic lunch, Lora joined Lew and the boys for the drive over to Ukiah.

"Happy hunting,"I called after them as they climbed in their car.

B.C. was rummaging in the refrigerator for a snack to tide her over until lunch when Frank Allen knocked on the screen door. "Came to get B.C. and to talk with you, Kay."

I let him in and waited for him to tell me what was on his mind. He took his time, going over to the cupboard and pouring himself a cup of coffee. While he stirred two lumps of sugar and doused cream in the cup, I studied his expressionless face.

Finally he looked up from his brew and said, "Kay, since you like to snoop, why not help us?"

Although irritated by his approach, I held my tongue.

Getting no response from me, Frank continued. "Maybe you heard on the news that the highway patrol found an abandoned dark blue car last night. It was a stolen car, but it had the license number agent, Ricky, spotted yesterday at the gas station where he met you and Ted."

"Good pilot,"I murmured. "Yes. we heard about the abandoned car but not about the license number."

Cutting off any further remarks of mine, Frank said, "Ricky reported on the two men right after you left with B.C. in the helicopter. He described them in detail and gave us the license number." When I didn't respond, he continued. "Obviously they had to get rid of the car before they were stopped for possessing stolen property." Frank toyed with his coffee cup before he asked, "Are you game to take a risk?"

"I'm not thrilled at the thought. What do you want me to do?"

"We need to find those men, and we'd like to use you as a lure."

"I'm not the siren type, Frank,"I said.

"Agreed, but we haven't anyone else right now."

"Flattering,"I muttered.

"Here's the deal. We've planted a story around town that

our agents may have left papers hidden in the Allison house. We want you to go there and search. This may draw those bums to the place."

"What do I say to them when they pull a gun on me?"

"Don't worry. We'll have our people surrounding the place."

"That's comforting. Do I just call out the window for help?"

"Be serious, Kay. First of all, our people will get a good look at the car the suspects are now driving and the disguises they may be using. If they don't threaten you, we'll let them get back in their car; and then we'll put a tail on them."

"And if they attack me?"

"You'll be wired, so you can reach us. OK?"

Ted would be furious when he learned about my snooping for the F.B.I. The thought of his anger decided me. "I'll do it. When do I start?"

"This afternoon. That should give enough time for the word to get around about the possible clues at the Allison house. I'll bring in what you'll need right now,"he said and went out to his car.

When he returned, he was carrying the paraphernalia I would need. Handing it to B.C., he told here to wire me. Before he left, he gave me specific instructions. "Take a bucket with you when you leave your house. Stop to pick berries along the way. Stroll into the Allison place."

"Is it locked?"

"No. Once inside, be alert for anyone hidden there. We'll be casing the outside of the grounds, but you won't see us."

"Just leaves crawling through the grass?"I asked.

He gave me an irritated look before continuing. "Act as if you are really searching. Look in drawers, behind curtains and pictures and under mattresses. You know the usual places."

"How long do I keep up this charade?"

"For a couple of hours. At the first sign of anyone there, press this button,"he said, pointing to the one at my side

After rehearsing me on the use of the wire, Frank and B.C.

climbed in his car.

"Be careful, Kay,"B.C. whispered to me.

"Good luck,"Frank said before shifting into drive and heading out to the highway.

As I stood staring at the retreating car, Julia came up behind me and said, "Let me go with you."

"Thanks for the offer, but I'd better do this alone. If Ted gets back before I do, you can tell him where I've gone." I was silent a moment then said, "I'm scared."

"You should be. Don't play the heroine. Punch that button at the first sign of trouble."

I was edgy the rest of the morning. I couldn't settle down to read or even pull out the trampoline to do a workout. In order to burn up some of my nervous energy, I scrubbed the kitchen floor and swept the porch. Over lunch I kept looking at the clock hands slowly move toward two o'clock. Enough waiting. I'd get this job over with as quickly as possible and maybe beat Ted and Eddie home.

A gentle breeze blew in from the ocean as I walked along, swinging my bucket. I hummed to myself, trying to stay calm. Occasionally I stopped to pick a few berries, popping most of them into my mouth. I peered in every car that passed me. Chipped Tooth and Whiny might be in one of them. However, I didn't see them. Only one person stopped to offer me a ride. That was the plumber who had recently overcharged us for a clogged drain.

When I reached the driveway leading to the Allison house, a squirrel darted across my path. Getting nuts for the winter, I supposed. As Frank had told me, the door was unlocked. Why hadn't they locked up after that examination of the place? I'd never understand the F.B.I., especially their agent, Frank Allen.

Before I turned the knob, I looked around for either Chipped Tooth or Whiny. I even looked up in the oak tree by the porch to see whether they or an agent was clinging to a branch and watching me. I saw nothing except bees sampling the honeysuckle by the steps.

Seeing no human being, I pushed open the door and walked

in. The place felt like any house that's been closed up for several days. I remembered coming home from vacations and throwing the windows open to freshen the air. Dust rose with each step I took, and I had a sneezing fit. A fly had accompanied me into the house and was now buzzing around the closed drapes.

"Anybody here?"I called out. "Silly. Just get on with your act,"I mumbled to myself.

Since I was in the hall, I carefully opened the closet door and waited. Nothing came out except the smell of moth balls. Turning on the flash light I'd remembered to bring along, I pushed back the few clothes hanging on the rod. A cricket chirped nearby. Suddenly I heard the scraping of a board. I stood broken, listening.

Hearing nothing further, I closed the closet door and told myself that old houses often creak, like aging people. Next I made my way to the kitchen, where there were still remains of the pizza Joe and Kent must have shared that last afternoon, before their fatal ride. Not even an ant wanted that stale food. You'd think the F.B.I. agents would have had the decency to clean up the table scraps.

I tried the cupboards. There were several cracked plates and a couple of cups. I smiled at the saucy girl on the calendar hanging beside the sink. She could have stood a few more clothes.

By now I was feeling brave. After a look in the bookshelves in the living room, I started toward the bedrooms. I never got there. I felt a sharp pain on the back of my head and gagged at the sickeningly sweet towel that covered my face. Then, oblivion.

CHAPTER FOURTEEN

When I awakened, it was pitch dark. My hands and feet wouldn't move. The ropes that bound them bit into my skin and hurt. My mouth was taped shut. Only my eyes and nose were free. I sniffed the stale air. Was I in a closet? While I tried to get used to the dark, a door next to me creaked open; and a beam of light assaulted my eyes.

"She's awake, Len,"a familiar whiny voice said.

I heard the scrape of a chair, then steps approaching. "Drag her out here, dummy, and dump her on the sofa," the other familiar voice - Chipped Tooth's - said.

Dummy or Whiny grabbed me by the shoulders and carried me like a sack of flour and dumped me on the dusty couch. I sneezed, then blinked, as a laser of light blinded me.

Chipped Tooth snorted, "Thought they'd use you as a decoy, did they? Fools!"

I tried to squeeze my elbows against the wire that was supposed to be there. The light followed my movements, and Chipped Tooth laughed.

"We got that stuff off you, while you were out,"he said.

I felt cold metal against my head.

"Yeah, it's a gun,"Chipped Tooth said. Turning to Whiny, he barked, "Pull that tape off her mouth, and you,"he said, tapping the gun against my head, "Don't yell. Just answer my questions."

Even after Whiny ripped the tape off my mouth, I said nothing, just stared at the two men.

"Seen enough? Now tell us what you're looking for," Chipped Tooth said.

I said nothing.

"Big choice, lady. Either you tell us, or I'll blow your brains out."

Anger welled up inside me at this threat. "And what will you find out, if you kill me?"

Chipped Tooth slapped me hard across the face. While I was reeling from the blow, I thought I saw lights flashing behind the heavy drapes. Before I could register what they meant, Chipped Tooth knocked me on the side of the head with the butt of his gun, and I fainted.

When I woke up this time, Whiny was leaning over me and wiping my face with a smelly wet cloth. "She's coming around, Len," he said.

Chipped Tooth pushed the other man out of the way and said, "Ready to talk?"

Before I could answer, I heard a welcome voice shout, "Freeze!"

In the melee that followed, I caught the sound of gun shots and shattered glass. Someone must have found the fuse box, because lights suddenly blazed in the house. B.C. ran to me and tried to cover my face while cutting the cords that bound me.

Nudging her hand away, I tried to sit up. When she cradled my back to support it, I stared at my two captors, now dead and sprawled at the foot of the couch. Waves of nausea swept over me. I lay back and let B.C. finish untying my hands and feet.

I heard pounding on the front door and Ted shouting, "Let me in, damn it!"

"OK, Ted, calm down and come get your wife," Frank Allen bawled out the window.

Ever gracious Frank!

Ted shoved Frank's agents aside and ran to me. When he picked me up, I curled in his arms and cried while he carried me outside. Gently lowering me to the ground, he began rubbing my bruised and partially numb hands and feet. Lew and Eddie came and knelt beside us.

"Julia told us where you were, and what Frank had asked you to do,"Lew said.

Ted interrupted his son and yelled at Frank, "You didn't give a shit about Kay, just catching the bad guys. Maybe they wouldn't kill the decoy, my wife."

A chagrined Frank had left the other agents and now stood beside us. When he started to speak, Ted waved him away. "Go clean up your mess inside the house and leave us alone."

"Wait a minute,"I managed to say through numbed lips. "I agreed to help Frank try to catch those two and knew I was taking a chance. Lay off Frank."

"Sorry, Frank, "Ted said. "All I could think of, while we stood outside waiting for your order to burst into the house, was Kay. Were the guys in there? Was Kay alive?"

"It was a damn risky thing I did," Frank said. "Still friends?"he asked holding out his hand to Ted.

Even though Ted nodded and shook hands with Frank, I could feel the anger and tension in my Ted. It would take time for the rift to heal. Frank must have felt it too as he looked at Ted, then slowly away..

When we saw Frank disappear into the house Lew said, "There was no car in sight when we got here. Frank spotted us and motioned for us to hide and wait."

"Soon he walked over to us and said he'd heard nothing in the house. Maybe the men hadn't shown up,"Eddie said, taking up the story. "

We'd wait a little longer hoping the creeps would appear."

Ted took up their tale. "When you didn't come out after an hour, I was frantic. Had something happened to you in the house? Had they come earlier and laid a trap? Were you all right? I ran over to Frank and begged him to go in. He wouldn't budge."

"Then we saw a flicker of light inside, and a tall shadow passed in front of the window. Too tall for you,"Lew said.

"It was then that Frank gave the signal, and his men rushed in,"Eddie said.

"And all hell broke loose inside,"Ted said, breaking in on Eddie's account.

While the three men were talking, Frank returned and handed Ted the keys to his FBI car. "It's parked in the gully behind the house," he said. Motioning toward me, he added, "Take her home. I'll be over as soon as I can get away if you'll let me darken your door."

Ted grimaced as he staggered to his feet, "Might even offer you a cup of poisoned coffee."

Was he having another heart attack, I wondered as I watched Ted lurch toward Frank's car. However, he straightened up after a few steps.

Turning to me, he said, "My legs fell asleep holding my favorite wife."

Was he still seething at Frank, or was he in pain? I couldn't tell.

Will and Tom raced out to meet us, when we braked in front of our place. "Did you catch the bad guys, Grandma?"Will asked.

"Sure did,"Lew told his sons while leading them up to the porch where Lora and Julia waited for us. Without saying a word, Lora embraced me. I could feel her tears on my face.

Julia broke the uncomfortable silence by saying, "I'll put the kettle on."

While I tried to wash the stench of the chloroform out of my mouth and nostrils and the dirt off me, Ted told the others what had happened at the Allison house. My head ached from the blows Chipped Tooth had given me. One eye was puffed and almost shut, and my cheek showed a nasty bruise.

When I came back in the living room, Frank was waiting for me. Tension was thick. Ted was leaning forward in his chair and shaking his fist at Frank. The children, sitting on the floor next to their dad, stared first at Ted, then at Frank. What had happened?

"She could have been killed,"Ted shouted. "But your little

game was the important thing, no matter who got hurt."

"Stop it, Ted,"I said and apologized to Frank for the outburst.

"I had it coming, Kay. There was no excuse for what happened at the Allison place."

At these words, Ted calmed down; and the tension in the room eased.

Lora and Lew slipped into the kitchen and put the stew on the stove after inviting Frank to stay for supper.

While we ate, Frank told us what had happened after we left. "The only thing we found on those two punks was a scrap of paper with a smeared letter - maybe an A or an O. We couldn't make it out." Frank took a bite of stew before continuing. "Funny thing was that the bullets that killed them didn't come from any of our guns or theirs."

"That's impossible,"Ted said.

"Not really. It means someone else wanted them dead. Who? It had to be someone right there with us,"Frank said.

"But who was there?"Ted said. "Your agents - how many of them were there? - and Lew and Eddie with me That's all."

"At least one more person,"Frank said. "Think hard. Did a neighbor join our wait? Remember, we were all hiding. When I gave the order to rush the house, there was chaos. Anybody could have gone in with us."

"And you needed Chipped Tooth and Whiny alive to wheedle information from them, didn't you?"I said. "Now that they are dead, what other leads do you have?"

Frank shrugged his shoulders and said, "None. It's back to square one. We have to find the ring leader."

"You think it's an organized groupinvolved,"Eddie asked.

"Yes. It's too well orchestrated to be a simple operation. First, the road accident, then the fire over at your neighbor's place and the attempt on Gilliam's life in the hospital." Looking over at me, Frank said, "Those two - what did you call them? Chipped Tooth and Whiny? They made a big mistake going into that house today. They had to be eliminated."

BETH HOWES

We were so engrossed in Frank's account that we didn't hear the footsteps on our porch. When someone knocked on the screen and called out, "Anybody home?"Eddie went to the front door and unlocked the screen.

"Glad to see you, Mr. Curtis. How is your wife?"he said.

"Still in shock from the fire. I sent her to her sister's in Omaha while I get our affairs in order." Glancing toward the screen, he added, "Glad to see you've started locking your door. I don't trust anyone since that fire."

"Sorry you lost everything in that fire, Mr. Curtis,"Frank said, getting up. "I hope you were insured."

Before our neighbor could answer, Frank turned to the rest of us and said we might be able to sit around talking, but he had worked to do.

Thanking us for the coffee, he waved his good bye and walked down the steps toward his car.

"Nice man,"Abe said, watching Frank drive out of our place. "He came by our lot while I was cleaning up the mess from the fire."Turning back to the rest of us, he let out a gasp, "What happened to you, Mrs. Roberts?"

"A little accident over at the Allison house,"I said, not wanting to talk about it.

"Allison house? I thought no one lived there. What happened?"Before I could speak, he said, "Wait a minute. I saw several cars over there today. I thought maybe someone had bought the place and we'd have new neighbors."

When I began to shake at the memory of my ordeal at the Allison house, Ted changed the subject. "Enough speculation about possible new neighbors. Leaning forward in his chair, Ted said, "Speaking of neighbors, what brings you out at this time of night, Abe?"

Giving us a sheepish grin Abe said, "I got scared of my own thoughts tonight and needed company." He hesitated, then added, "I keep hearing the explosion and then see the flames leaping up all around our house. I had to talk to someone."

"I'm glad you came, Abe. Is there anything we can do for

you?"Ted said.

"Just be here, I guess, and maybe give me some advice."

"Advice?" About what?"

"About the property. Should I sell it? Rebuild?"

We listened as Abe shared his feelings about the place. This was the home he and Alice had planned to stay in the rest of their lives. Should they leave and start a new life elsewhere?

It was almost midnight before Abe left and we settled down for the night. The sleeping pill Ted gave me was beginning to ease the pain in my head as I climbed into bed. Within a few minutes I was fast asleep and heard nothing until I awoke to the smell of coffee and bacon the next morning.

Reaching over to Ted's side of the bed, I found it empty. When I opened my eyes, I saw the note he had put on his pillow.

"Eddie and I've gone out to photograph north of here. See you around noon."

I jumped out of bed and ran to the shower. Nine o'clock already and I never sleep past seven. One look in the mirror told me I wasn't top drawer this morning. My cheek was swollen and my eye a bruised slit. When I touched the back of my head, I winced. Yesterday's adventure was one I didn't want to think about. When I went to the kitchen, Lora was loading the dishwasher.

"Sorry you missed breakfast, Mom. My bacon didn't burn for once. Want me to try my luck with a couple of rashers for you?"

When I shook my head, she said, "Frank Allen stopped by and took Julia up to visit her husband. Lew's taken the boys to find our two camera buffs."

Sipping the coffee Lora poured for me, I said, "They're not trying to swing in space like their Uncle Eddie, are they?"

"No. They took the road up to the post office first, then were coming back to look for a place to get down to the beach to see Uncle Eddie make his way down a cliff side."

"Crazy way to make a living, isn't it?"I said, and added, "Ted's note said he and Eddie would be working north of here. Lew could get down near the Curtis place." I was feeling restless "Let's go find them. If the boys can inch their way toward the beach, we can too. Come on."

We didn't have any trouble locating where Lew and the boys had gone through the fence. I caught sight of Will's red cap stuck on some berry bushes beside the road. Lora and I jumped across the ditch separating the road from the bushes and the barbed wire fence.

"Ouch,"I cried, as my hands landed on one of the prickly vines. Getting up and pulling a thorn out of my hand, I climbed over the fence which Lora held down for me. When I returned the favor, she stepped over the barbed wire with much more grace than I had mustered. The sea lions were barking to each other and drowning out the sound of voices or of the waves breaking over the shore a few hundred yards ahead of us.

When we came to a clearing, I looked down and saw Eddie swinging on the rope Ted was holding. Eddie was yelling something we couldn't hear. Ted lowered the rope to what must have been a ledge a few feet down the side. Focusing his camera, Eddie took several pictures, then pulled on the rope. Ted began reeling it in.

We couldn't see the boys from this spot. Soon we found the road leading to Abe Curtis' place and walked in comparative ease the rest of the way to where his house once stood.

"There they are,"Lora cried, pointing to a clump of bushes that had escaped the fire.

When I spied them, the three of them were down on their knees and seemed to be following something on the ground. As Lora and I walked toward them, we saw new markers on the property. Lew was following one out toward the sea while Will and Tom were crawling along an area to the north.

When I looked back and tried to locate Ted and Eddie again, I froze. In the distance I could see someone was watching us. I tried to warn Lora, but no sound came from my throat. I heard a shot. A bullet whined by Lora's head and landed in front of her. She whirled around. I ran to her, and we dropped to the ground. There was no protection for us here in the open.

I raised my head and saw Lew hurrying toward us. The boys, on their short legs, were running to catch up with their father.

"Get over near that tree,"Lew yelled, and pointed.

When we were all out of the sniper's range, I looked back at the spot where I had seen the man. No one was there. Where had he gone? Was he stalking Eddie and Ted? Eddie would be an easy target when he was dangling in space over the ravine. Ted could be shot from behind. With no one holding the rope, Eddie would plummet to the rocks below.

CHAPTER FIFTEEN

"Get the boys out of here," I said to Lora. "Lew and I'll try to warn Ted and Eddie."

"Mom, are you crazy? You'll be killed!" Lora grabbed Will's and Tom's hands and started toward the highway. "Come on, Mom. You too, Lew."

It was then that I saw Abe Curtis turn into his driveway. He stopped walking and stared at us. Before we could explain, he said, "What is this, a social call?"

"Didn't you hear the shot?" Lew asked and added, "Better take cover, Abe."

"What shot?" Abe asked looking all around his burned out property. "Wasn't the fire enough to destroy Alice and me?"

"Some sniper's loose. Almost got Lora."

"Sniper? That's ridiculous. Probably a hunter thought he could bag a deer while I was gone," Abe said as he walked toward us.

"Maybe he's zeroing in on Ted and Eddie right now, " I said. "Come on; we have to warn them."

"Where are they?" Abe asked.

"Down in that ravine somewhere north of here. Help us get to them, Abe," Lew said.

"Damned poacher," Abe muttered as he followed Lew down a slope toward the sea. The rest of us tagged along behind them.

"There they are," I shouted, when I looked across the ravine and saw Eddie safely reach the beach. While I watched, he untied his rope and jumped across the little stream that separated Abe's property from that to the north of him. When Eddie looked up to signal to Ted, he saw us and waved. He seemed to be yelling something to us, but we couldn't hear him over the roar of the sea lions.

"Where's Ted?" Abe asked. "He didn't fire that shot, did he?"

"At his own family?" I snorted.

" From the way Eddie is signaling, Dad should be somewhere on the other side of the creek." Pointing in the opposite direction, Lew added, "And the shot came from those bushes on this side of your property. Didn't you see anyone when you were walking along the highway?"

"Only a biker puffing up the hill. He sure wasn't toting a rifle," Abe said.

"Maybe some other kind of gun," I suggested.

"Well, he wasn't waving it around for me to see," Abe said. Relaxing now that there were no further shots whizzing by our heads, he grinned and said, "I thought you were trespassers, crazies come to cart off remains from the fire. Mighty poor pickings! There have been some weird ones sniffing around here the last few days."

As we walked down the sloping land toward Eddie, we heard someone crashing through the roadside brambles and moving toward us.

Terrified, we stopped and waited until we heard a welcome voice. Ted's.

"Grandpa," Will and Tom shouted and ran to him. Shifting the rope he had looped over his shoulder, Ted stooped down and waited for their embrace. I felt weak with relief.

"What is this, a convention?" Ted asked. "Did you invite all these folks to help you clean up, Abe?"

"I could sure use their help, but they came looking for you,"

"And nearly got shot," I said and told Ted about the sniper.

"They even thought I'd fired the shot, thinking they were

trespassers. Some day I'll learn to wear my glasses, when I'm awake. Don't want to fire at friends."

"Funny, I didn't hear any shot,"Ted said, putting down his gear and easing to the ground.

"Too far away, probably,"Abe said. He hesitated before continuing. "By the way, why are you folks here? Come for a visit?"

"Trespassing,"Lew said. We came to find our fellow trespassers, Dad and Eddie."

"I'm sorry, Abe. I should have come over and told you that Eddie and I are doing a job for Eddie's company - photographing oceanside lots for several miles around here. Forgive us?"

"Forgiven, but why does his company want this done and on this stretch of land?"

"I honestly don't know why,"Ted said. "But maybe your property will appear in one of those glossy magazines you leaf through in the dentist's or doctor's office. Wish you had a house to show in the photos."

"You probably couldn't have found me, even if you'd come to ask leave to cross my land. After I took Alice in Harry's little hopper to San Francisco to catch her plane to Omaha, Harry insisted that I stay with him." Abe let out a sigh and glanced at the chimney, the one reminder still standing where his house had been. "I did impose on you good neighbors the other night when I came by to look at my place. The lights from your house were too inviting for this lonely man."

"Why not come over and have supper with us tonight?"I asked. "Make up for our barging onto your land uninvited."

A big smile played across Abe's face as he asked, "When do we eat?"

"Six o'clock,"I said. "How does fresh caught fish sound to you?"

"Mighty tasty. I'll be there." Bending down to listen to a wiggling Tom, who was pulling on Abe's pant legs, he asked, "What is it, son?"

"Mr. Curtis, what are those markers stuck in the

ground?"Tom asked.

"Markers? Oh, those are the ones the insurance company used to determine my exact property line. Said it was necessary in settling my claim for the fire the other night."

As Abe spoke, I saw a puzzled look on Lew's face. On the way back to our house, I caught up with him and said, "What's bothering you?"

"That business about the markers for insurance purposes. It's probably true, but I found there was action on Abe's property several months ago, long before the fire."

"You learned that from the County Clerk's office, did you?"Ted asked, coming up to join Lew and me.

Lew nodded. "That and the fact that someone's been inquiring about the land parcels on both sides of Abe's property, including yours."

"Ours?"I asked, feeling a chill at the thought of someone checking on our place.

Lew, oblivious to my fear, went on talking about his time at the Court House. "I was lucky. The clerk was real chatty and mentioned the guys who had asked for information on all three lots; Abe's, the one to the north of his, and yours. Three different persons came inquiring. I was the fourth, she said. No, she had never seen any of them before, including me, she added with a laugh."

Before we could talk further, we heard a shout behind us. Eddie came racing past us carrying Tom on his shoulders. Will was close on his heels and crying, "It's my turn." When we looked back, Lora, loaded with Eddie's camera, was standing in the middle of the road and laughing.

"Come up and join us, camera woman,"Lew said, walking back to meet his wife. "What's that brother of mine doing?"

"Giving camel rides. Want one?"

"No, I'll wait to ride the real thing,"he said, squeezing her hand.

Over dinner that night we asked Abe Curtis whether he had heard from Alice. Yes, she had phoned from Omaha and left a message at Harry's house for Abe.

"You know, as close as we live to one another, we haven't been real neighborly,"Ted said, handing Abe the fish platter. "Just exchanged greetings when we met at the post office or the store."

"I remember when you folks moved into this place. About five years ago, wasn't it?"

Ted nodded, and Abe continued. "We came out from the Middle West when I retired the year before you came. We wanted to forget big city life and crawl into our shells for a while."

"What kind of work did you do?"Lew asked.

"Public relations for a chemical company with headquarters in Chicago. But I spent most of my time in the air, flying to London, Paris, Rome. It was exciting but wearing. Umm, this is good," he said as he reached for another ear of corn.

While Abe ate his way around the rows of corn kernels, Ted told him about our family.

Over coffee Abe talked about his options. He and Alice didn't know whether to rebuild or sell. He'd had offers he said. "And even threats, as you know."

When the clock struck nine, Abe got up to leave. "Enough of my problems. Thanks for a good meal and, remember, you can traipse across my land any time, but watch out for the sniper."

"We'll send you a copy of any good photo we get of your place,"Eddie said, walking Abe to the door.

After locking up for the night, Eddie said, "Are you ready for another day of photographing, Dad?"

"Sure. If we're on Abe's property, I can stay with you and carry some of your gear. No need for the rope on that flat ground, is there?"

"I don't think so, but we may finish sooner there and be ready to move onto the next lot, so you'd better bring the rope." Eddie's face brightened as he said, "How would you like to swing out in space, Dad? I can rope you in,"

"Not on your life,"I said, glaring at both Ted and Eddie.

"Just kidding, Mom,"my daredevil son said. "How about you? Want to try it?"

"No way, I answered as he picked me up and whirled me around the room. "Put me down and save your energy for your work tomorrow,"I added and kissed him good night.

While we were getting ready for bed, we heard a car brake in front of our place and light steps coming up on the porch.

"It's me, Julia,"a voice said after we heard a light knocking on the door.

"Sorry, we locked you out,"I said, letting her in. "How's Joe?"

"Well enough to travel. I'll take him home for a vacation tomorrow." As I started to open her sofa bed, Julia came up and put her arms around me. "Thanks for taking me in. You folks are wonderful."

I liked her sentiment.

While we were eating breakfast the next morning, Frank Allen came to pick up Julia. He ignored our questions about Joe's fishing gear except to say that he had found it in the truck. As usual, I was irritated by his lack of trust in us.

As Julia and Frank were leaving, B.C. rounded the side of the house and came in to say goodbye to Julia. Turning back to us, she said, "Bacon smells good. May I have some?"

Laughing at our always hungry friend, I took her into the kitchen with me and put the bacon on to fry.

When Ted and Eddie picked up the camera and rope to begin their morning of photographing, Lew volunteered to walk along with them to the Curtis place where they would continue their work.

Taking Lora's hand he called to his sons, "Come on, boys. The four of us will tag along with Grandpa and Uncle Eddie; watch them crawl under the wire fence over at Mr. Curtis; then go pick up the mail and the newspaper."

Will let out a whoop and, with Tom close on his heels, raced down the steps and out toward the road. Suddenly the house was blessedly quiet. While I refilled our coffee cups, B.C. began talking about her family.

"Mom's back in the hospital, and Dad needs help,"she said.

Coming back to the table and handing B.C. her cup, I said, "Tell me about them. You've never mentioned them before."

"We're not supposed to talk about anything personal when we're on duty, Kay,"B.C. said. She stopped speaking and searched in her pocket for a tissue. Tears rolled down her cheeks.

I handed her a box of tissues and waited for her to continue.

"I've put in for a month's leave. Frank's working on it and promises he can release me by the end of the week. What if I'm too late for Mom?" She put her head down on the table and sobbed.

I reached over and took her hand. "Come on. Let's phone your dad right now." When she hesitated, I said, "What's the number?" As soon as I had her dad on the line, I handed her the phone and left the room. They needed privacy.

Several minutes later B.C. came out on the porch to sit with me. "Mom had a good night, Dad says. When I told him I'd probably be home for a month, he brightened up and said that was the best medicine for Mom." B.C. choked back a sob and added, "Dad sounded so helpless. His last words were, 'I need you, daughter.'" Getting up from her chair, she said, "Enough about my troubles. Back to headquarters to make my report, then I'll climb in the sack for a good eight hours of sleep."

"Thanks for sharing with me, B.C.,"I said. "After all, I feel as close to you as a sister."

She hugged me but was too moved to say anything.

I watched her stride up our driveway and wait at the highway until a motorcycle braked in front of her. She hopped on and waved to me, as the cyclist revved the motor and took off.

I was putting away my trampoline and reaching for yesterday's crossword puzzle when Lora and Lew mounted the steps and sank into chairs beside me.

"Usual bad new in the headlines, Mom,"Lew said, spreading out the front section of the paper for me to see. "An uprising in Eastern Europe, a hurricane moving toward the Florida Coast, Congress stalled over the budget. Still want to read the paper?"

"Sure. Keeps the old adrenalin flowing." I reached for the paper.

"Where are the boys?"Lora asked, looking in the kitchen and down the hall.

"Didn't they stay with you?"

"Yes, until we came to Abe's place. Then they darted under the fence and called out that they would look for Grandpa and Uncle Eddie and catch up with us."

Her face turned ashen as she added, "But they never caught up with us. We thought they might have taken a short cut to your place."

"There is no short cut,"I said and froze at the thought of the boys being missing.

Lew jumped to his feet and ran toward the road. "Will, Tom,"he shouted as he sped up our driveway.

Lora and I raced behind him calling out to the boys. Gasping for breath, I stopped to check the bushes on the other side of the ditch along the road. Maybe they were playing hide and seek down in the ditch or behind one of the thick berry bushes.

"Will, Tom,"I called in a quavering voice. "Game's up. Come on out from the bushes." No answer. There was no giggle or footstep, except for my own crunching on the dry grass and trailing vines of the berry bushes. Lew and Lora had disappeared around a curve in the road. I continued calling to the boys until I reached the Curtis property.

Lifting the barbed wire, I crawled under the fence. As I got to my feet and dusted off my hands, I heard Lew calling to his sons. No response. When I came to the burned out clearing, I saw Ted and Eddie working along the northern edge of Abe's property. I ran down the slope toward them, as Lora emerged from the southern end of the Curtis holdings. She was stumbling along and sobbing.

Both Eddie and Ted had their backs to me. Eddie was kneeling on a wet strip of sand and stones and focusing his camera. Ted was holding the rope and other gear away from the fingers of the incoming tide.

When I was close enough for them to hear, I shouted, "Ted, have you seen Will and Tom?"

Ted jerked around and stared at me. "Will and Tom? No.

What's wrong?" Clutching the rope and camera equipment, he ran to meet me. I almost fell into his arms.

Before I could speak, Lora caught up with us. "They're gone, Dad,"she cried.

CHAPTER SIXTEEN

Eddie, with his camera slung over his shoulder, joined us. "Steady, Lora. We'll find them," he said and asked, "What happened?"

Between sobs, Lora said, "Will and Tom were playing tag all the way from the post office. When we got to the Curtis place, they crawled under the fence and said they were going to look for you two. They promised to catch up with us after seeing you, but they never did."

"Where's Lew?"

Before Lora could answer, we saw Lew beckoning to us. Without a word we ran to him.

"They've been here, all right. Look at this,"he said, holding up the red cap Tom had been wearing this morning.

Lora choked back a sob as she grabbed the hat. While the rest of us stared at the hat, too stunned to act, Ted took charge.

"No sense standing here gaping at the hat. You, Eddie, check the creek on the south side of the property. Lew, show me where you found the hat, and we'll track the ground along there."

When I looked out at the ocean, Ted said, "We'd have seen them, if they had come down to the water's edge, Kay. You and Lora search near the fence for any signs of the boys. We'll meet at the house chimney in fifteen minutes. If they don't turn up, we call the sheriff. Get going, all of you."

Eddie took off for the creek, while Lora and I scrambled up

to the fence. Getting down on our hands and knees, we searched the length of the property, then inched down toward the scorched earth where the house had stood a few days ago. There was no sign of Tom or Will. When we reached the chimney, Eddie was waiting for us.

Ted and Lew emerged from a thicket at the edge of the charred earth.

"Will's shoe!"Lora screamed as she saw what Lew held in his hand.

Lew was shaking as he nodded. Just then we heard a truck bumping along the rutted road leading to the burned out house. As we stood rooted to the spot near the chimney, Abe Curtis braked and jumped out.

"Trespassing again?"he said and laughed. When no one answered him, he said, "What's the matter? You look as if you've lost your best friend."

Lora broke down and cried.

"What is it?"Abe asked, slamming the truck door and hurrying over to us.

When Lew told him about the boys, Abe said, "I'll get the sheriff on my C.B. You'll want to talk to him, Lew."

While Abe and Lew were walking to the truck, I whispered to Ted, "I'll need a ride to our place to call Frank Allen." Ted nodded and caught up with Abe.

"Mind dropping the women back at our place after you reach the sheriff, Abe? Someone had better watch for the boys there,"Ted said.

"Sure. Bet the scamps are already back there."

When Lew finished reporting to the sheriff, he climbed down from the cab of the truck and thanked Abe. "The sheriff's deputy will be here shortly. He's rounding up more help in hunting for the boys." Going over to Lora, he put his arm around her and said, "We'll find them, honey." Seeing the gray pallor in Ted's face, Lew said, "Why don't you go back with Mom and Lora, Dad? Eddie and I'll wait for the sheriff's crew."

"Not much I can do here, so I'll take your camera and the

other gear back to the house with me, Eddie,"Ted said, tossing the equipment in the back of the truck and climbing in with it. "If the boys show up, I'll phone the sheriff's office and walk over to give you the good news."

"Hop in, Kay and Lora,"Abe said, getting into the driver's seat and turning on the engine.

I held Lora's cold hand as we rode the short distance to our place. As soon as we stopped in front of the house, she opened the truck door and jumped out.

"Will? Tom?"she called as she ran up the steps and into the house. Thank goodness I had forgotten to lock the front door.

Abe waited a few minutes to see whether the boys had returned. When Lora got no answer to her calls and we saw no one, Abe left us, saying, "With all of us looking, we'll find the youngsters."

I scurried up the steps and over to the phone in the living room. I mumbled the phone number to myself as I dialed Frank Allen. Frank answered on the first ring.

"At the house, are you? I'll be right over. Stay put,"he said, and slammed down the receiver.

While I waited on the porch with Ted, I suddenly thought of our tiny beach. The tide was coming in. Maybe the boys had wandered down there, looking for us. God, I hoped not. Ted wanted to go with me, but one look at his gray color told me he shouldn't attempt it today.

"One of us needs to stay with Lora. Don't let her come down to the cove or even know I'm there. She'd be frantic." When Ted started to argue with me and insist that he go in my place, I reminded him that he was Lora's favorite and that she would do what he felt best. Reluctantly Ted agreed to stay at the house and keep Lora company.

I went to the edge of the cliff and began my descent. The wind whipped strands of my hair across my face as I inched from toehold to toehold. At last I reached the bottom. The tide was almost at its peak. Only a few yards of our stony beach was exposed. Seaweed floated near one of my usual tide pools, now under water. Keeping an eye on the sea, I felt around for any scrap that might tell me the boys had been here. I found nothing.

When my shoes filled with water, I squished over the slippery rocks to the steps and made my way back to the top of the cliff. Lora ran to me as I climbed the last step and started toward the house.

She stopped and stared at my wet shoes and cried out, "Oh, no!"

"Stop it, Lora. They are not down there, and there is no sign that they have been there."

Before she could answer, Frank Allen careened into our driveway. "Tell me everything from the last moment you saw the boys,"he demanded as he stepped onto our porch.

When we finished our accounts, he brushed past us and used our phone. "All points alert. House to house check-all harbor activity-road blocks. Any airplane or helicopter activity in the last two hours,"he said and slammed down the receiver.

"Kidnaped?"I whispered as he passed me on his way out the door.

"Might be,"he said and disappeared among the trees.

"Where's he going, Mom, and what were the two of you saying?"Lora asked, coming up behind me.

"He's probably checking our security. Maybe one of his team saw the boys,"I said, ignoring her second question.

"Mom, did I hear the word (kidnapped)?"

When I didn't answer, she shrieked, "Kidnapped! That's it! Road, harbor and air check. House to house search. My boys! That's it. He thinks they've been kidnapped!"

She was screaming and shaking so hard, it took both Ted and me to calm her down. "Maybe they are dead, just like the baby boy I lost at the hospital a few days ago." While she was keening over this possibility and the recent loss of the fetus, Frank reappeared.

"My agents on duty have seen nothing, but they are scouring every inch of the land around here for any clue." While he was reporting to us, Frank's beeper squawked to life. "Frank here."he said and listened. "Thanks,"he said, and disconnected.

Turning to us, he said, "There's a possible break. The local weather man on his morning surveillance spotted some commotion north of here. On the Curtis property, he thinks. He figured folks were just clearing out from the fire, so he didn't report it. A couple of bundles were being lifted into a truck when the weather man passed overhead. He couldn't see the faces of the people on the ground but assumed they were a work crew."

Hearing this, Lora fainted.

"Get a cool, damp rag, Kay, while I carry her to the couch,"Frank said, lifting the limp figure and depositing her on the sofa.

"A real bedside manner,"I grumbled. "She's still recovering from her miscarriage. Remember?"

Frank ignored my comments.

A few minutes later Lora sputtered awake and wiped the drops of water off her face. "Sorry, Mom,"she said, forcing herself to sit up. "What do we do now?"

"Wait and hope,"Frank said as we heard a car out front.

I went to the door and saw our neighbor, Harry Burns, walking toward our porch.

After greeting me, he said, "What's going on around here? I went out to the airport to service my plane, and the place was crawling with strangers. Someone said a couple of kids are missing - the Roberts boys."

"Our grandsons, Harry. We're frantic,"I said, holding the screen door open for him.

"Oops, sorry. I didn't mean to butt in,"he said when he saw Lora and Frank in the room.

"Good to see you, Harry,"Ted said, getting up and coming to shake hands with him. Looking over at Lora, he added, "Harry is the neighbor who's offered to fly Mom and me out of here in an emergency. Ticker trouble and the like." Pointing to Frank, he said, "And, Harry, this is Frank Allen."

Before Ted could say more, Frank interrupted. "You must be the man who has that little four-seater out at the airport. Care to help us in our search?"

"Glad to. What do you want me to do?"Harry answered.

"No sense standing around here stewing. Go on out to the airport. I'll follow you and give you instructions as soon as we get there,"Frank said, before stalking out of the house and slamming the screen door.

"Old affable Frank,"I said to an astonished Harry. "Thanks for your help. We need it."

"I'll come with you and be another set of eyes in your plane,"Ted said, grabbing his bird watching glasses and following Harry to the car. As the two cars sped away, I turned to Lora and said, "Frank will never be crowned Mr. Congeniality, but he's one of the best investigators in the business. He'll find our boys, Lora."

"I hope so,"she murmured.

I glanced at my watch and said, "Maybe there's something on the noon news."

Lora jumped up and ran to the TV. I turned on the radio and dialed the news station. There was nothing about our missing boys or the search on either set.

Refusing to eat anything, Lora said she wanted to lie down. "Call me, Mom, if you hear anything,"she said as she walked down the hall toward her bedroom.

"Sure. Try to sleep. I'll call you if anything breaks,"I said.

I picked up a magazine, but the words swam before my eyes. I couldn't concentrate. To calm myself, I pulled out a deck of cards and began a game of solitaire. While I played a black queen on a red king and shuffled the cards, I tried to think of any place the boys might be hidden. Had Frank and his agents checked the Allison house, I wondered. That would be one of the first places they would look. I shuddered as I heard the waves crash on the rocks below. No, the boys wouldn't be washed out to sea. I felt so helpless.

I walked out on the porch. Wisps of fog were beginning to cover the sun as it moved closer to the horizon. How long would the team continue the hunt if the fog closed in on us? I stifled a sob, picturing the boys lying in some lonely place and feeling hungry and scared.

Lora came out to join me. Her eyes were red from crying. No sense in asking her whether she had slept. I had no comforting words to give her. While we sat staring out to sea, the telephone rang. We raced to the phone. Lora picked it up and said, "Roberts residence," then listened and held the phone so that I could hear.

"They are safe,"a muffled voice said. "Tomorrow morning,"and the caller hung up.

We grabbed one another and cried. In the midst of our joy that the boys were safe, nagging questions arose.

"Where are they?"Lora asked. "How do we know they are safe?"

I had no answer. And where would we find them tomorrow morning?

We were asking each other these questions when we heard cars driving into our lane. Lew and Eddie were in the back of Frank's car, and Ted was up front in Abe Curtis' truck. When she saw Lew, Lora ran to him and told him about the phone call. Ted, looking weary, held me in his arms when I went down the steps to him.

"Safe. Tomorrow morning,"Frank repeated the words of the caller. For once Frank seemed perplexed. What could he and the sheriff's deputies do? Nothing but wait. Shaking his head he said, "Someone will phone again with instructions. We'll try to intercept them when they drop the boys."

"No, you won't,"Lew shouted. "Don't you risk our boys' lives. Didn't you almost get our mother killed with your bungling?"

"Enough, Lew,"Ted said, touching his son's arm. "Frank's our friend." Turning to Frank, Ted asked, "What's your plan?"

"I wish I had one. Right now I'm stumped. There's been no ransom demand. We don't know where the party will leave the boys. Maybe the next call will clear up a few things." With these words Frank walked over to the edge of the cliff and looked out to sea.

I had never before seen him lose control of a situation. When one of his agents came over to him, I saw Frank shake his head and continue to stare toward the horizon.

Although the thought of food made me nauseated, I managed, with Ted's help, to make sandwiches for the others. Only Abe Curtis ate with gusto. Snatching a second sandwich, he walked out and offered it to Frank who shook his head and continued to lean on the fence and look out to sea.

A few minutes later I saw Frank walk to his car and drive away. A puzzled Abe came back in the house to thank me for feeding him. "That Frank's a strange man. Refused to eat. Wouldn't talk. No expression on his face."

"He's a deeply caring man,"I said before taking a sip of the hot tea Eddie had brought me.

As Abe was preparing to leave, he said, "By the way, I'm staying on with Harry Burns a while longer. Maybe I'll get me a trailer and move it on my property while I'm deciding whether or not to rebuild."

"How does your wife, Alice, feel about rebuilding?"I asked.

"She hasn't said, and I'm not sure she will be happy staying at Harry's place. But can she stand looking at the shell of our old house? I just don't know what to do!" Giving a little sigh, Abe said, "No sense burdening you with my troubles. I'll see you folks later,"he added and went out to his car and drove away.

We didn't hear the usual sound of the motorcycle dropping off our guards, but we soon heard the whistle as the next crew took over the watch.

Although it was the middle of the afternoon, fog had almost blocked out the sun. It didn't usually roll in this early. I was tucking the sandwich makings back in the refrigerator when I heard a knock on the screen door.

There was Frank Allen peering through the screen and giving me a sheepish grin.

"Care to have a lodger tonight?"he asked.

"Who?"

"Me. Fog's too thick for safe driving."

"An F.B.I. man who can't see through the fog? I'm disappointed."

"This way you can sting me with your sharp tongue and ask your snoopy questions all evening unless the fog lifts,"Frank said. "Besides, I might not be able to get back tomorrow morning to help with the rescue of your grandsons."

"No chance of the fog's lifting until mid morning. Think you can stand being at my mercy that long?"

"I'll try,"he said, giving me a wry smile.

None of us was up to witty conversation that night. After listening to the ten o'clock news we drifted off to our beds. Frank was already snoring on the sofa bed in the living room when I turned off my reading light and fell asleep.

When I wakened the next morning, the fog was already starting to dissipate. Putting on my jeans, I hurried out to the kitchen to start the coffee maker. There was no need to tiptoe though the living room. The sofa bed was folded up, and Frank Allen was nowhere in sight.

I was measuring the coffee when the phone rang. Dropping the coffee can on the counter, I ran to the phone; but Lew beat me to it.

"Our cove? When?" Lew listened, hung up and raced out of the house. I ran after him. Lora was right behind me. As I felt for the first step leading to the beach, I saw Frank's crew zeroing in on our cove.

By the time I reached the rocks below, Frank and B.C. were swimming out into the incoming tide toward a raft. Horrified, I saw Will and Tom crouching in it. As I watched, Frank and B.C. reached the raft. Fighting against the turbulent waves, they grabbed the raft and started the perilous swim back to shore.

CHAPTER SEVENTEEN

Eddie, barefooted, stood on shore waiting for the raft to get closer. Seconds later Lew joined him, and the two of them waded into the surf to lift the sobbing children to safety. Members of Frank's team were swarming over the beach, and a helicopter hovered overhead.

Lora stumbled over the rocks and grabbed Tom from Eddie's arms, while Lew carried Will to drier ground. By the time I reached them, they were removing the blindfolds from the boys' eyes and murmuring reassuring words to their sons.

Dropping down on the wet stones beside them, I wept with relief. When I reached over and stroked their matted wet hair, they whimpered and buried their faces in their parents' shoulders. In minutes they were asleep. Glancing up, I saw Eddie moving among the search team and taking pictures. Where was Ted?

When Eddie finished his photographing, he came over and took Tom from Lora and handed her his camera. As he and Lew began carrying the boys toward the cliff steps, I heard the helicopter's pilot bawl out through his bull horn, "Stay where you are. I'll drop a basket for the boys and put them up on high ground for you."

Lora and I caught the basket as it swayed between us and the cliff steps and held it while Lew and Eddie placed the sleeping youngsters in it. Slowly the pilot lifted the basket up from the cove and waited for the four of us to climb the steps to retrieve the boys.

Before starting on my upward journey, I looked around for Ted. Worried, I called up to Eddie who was on the rung above me, "Have you seen your father?"

"Not since Frank and he were talking together on the beach before the rescue." Eddie stopped to catch his breath before continuing. "Frank may have given Dad an assignment, so don't worry about him, Mom."

Of course I'd worry about Ted until I knew he was all right. As I stepped on firm ground at the top of the cliff, I saw Lew and Eddie go over to the waiting helicopter and take the boys in their arms.

"Thanks!" Lew shouted to the pilot who waved and disappeared. I was still puffing from the climb, when the helicopter reappeared and deposited its second pair of passengers, B.C. and Frank. In spite of their dripping clothes, I ran to B.C. and hugged her and even gave Frank a kiss.

"You two are wonderful," I gushed, as cold droplets of salt water dribbled down my arms. Walking beside them back to our house, I asked Frank, "Do you know where Ted is?"

"Sure. Oh, my gosh, I forgot about him in all the excitement. I sent him up to the highway to watch for the kidnappers in case they tried to escape us." Pulling his watertight beeper from his pocket, he barked an order to one of his crew to go relieve Ted. "Tell him we have the boys but no kidnappers." Turning to me, he said, "Any old towels B.C. and I can drape around ourselves while our clothes dry?"

"We'll find something," I said and walked with them the rest of the way to our place. Lew and Eddie came out of the boys' bedroom and came over to join me in the Living room. Lora was going to stay with Will and Tom.

"They have had enough of a scare, and she doesn't want them terrified by waking up in an empty room," Lew said.

"Good thinking," I said as Frank, wrapped in one of Ted's old robes, stuck his head into the living room.

"Ready for a fashion show?" he asked. Without waiting for our answers, he strolled in and draped himself in a chair. "I'll tell you what I know happened. B.C. can fill in other details, I'm sure."

When he saw me glance toward the boys' room, he said, "Don't bother to waken them. They need their sleep."

"Start at the beginning for us, Frank,"Lew said. "About first spotting the boys."

"They had been sedated, as you know. And they are still groggy from the drug. Thank goodness, they were blindfolded. They would have been terrified to see nothing but the ocean churning around the raft." Frank shifted in his chair and pulled Ted's robe more modestly around himself before continuing.

"When the team, including Ted and you guys, first went down to the cove to wait, we could see nothing. Then the fog started to lift. In the murky light my agents checked every possible hiding place—overhangs, trees clinging to the hillside and outgrowth on the cliff. Nothing. When the sun burned off more of the fog, I heard the churning of a chopper overhead, then a splash. I immediately sent Ted topside to cover the highway. That might have been the kidnappers' way of escape."

Ted! Where was Ted?

"Then, through a break in the fog, I saw a helicopter lifting someone up and taking off. They had dropped something in the water. One of my men shouted, 'Get the raft'. There, bobbing in the ocean, was an oar- less raft. Two heads appeared over the edge. Without thinking, B.C. and I stripped to the bare necessities and dived into the ocean. We had to get that raft before it was carried out to sea. Thanks to the incoming tide, we were able to pull it to shore. You know the rest of the story."

While we were absorbing Frank's tale, one of his agents with a body slung over his shoulder, mounted the porch steps. Frank jumped to his feet and ran out the door. "My God! Ted! Is he dead?"

I leaped to my feet and, shoving Lew aside, ran to Ted.

"He will be all right, ma'am. Just been knocked out,"the agent said.

I ignored him and began keening, "Ted, Ted, " while rubbing his cold face.

"I found him in the ditch at the side of the road, sir,"the agent said to Frank. " He has a nasty wound, still bleeding, on the back of his head, but he's coming around."

"Here, put him on the couch,"Frank said as the others moved aside for Ted and his rescuer. Turning to the rest of us, Frank said, "Don't just stand there. Get some bandages and some warm soapy water to clean him up. And he'll need some hot tea or coffee to drink and an ice pack for his head."

The others scurried to carry out Frank's orders, but I knelt beside Ted and continued murmuring to him and caressing his forehead. When Eddie handed me a pan of warm water and a wash cloth, I began bathing Ted's face. Before long he opened his eyes and tried to focus on me.

When he moved his head, he groaned, "Ouch! My head. What happened?"

"You've had a little accident, fella,"Frank said, gently shifting Ted on his side and cleaning out the deep gash on the back of Ted's head. "Where's that disinfectant?"he asked, holding out his hand for the bottle.

Ted winced, as the medication stung his wound. When Ted rolled on his back, he cried out with pain and fainted.

Worried about a possible concussion, Frank said, "No sleeping, Ted. Damn it, where's the ice pack and get me some cold water to bring him around. Do I have to think of everything?"

"Here, sir,"one of his agents said, handing Frank a small glass of water.

We watched Frank sprinkle a few drops on Ted's forehead, wait, and sprinkle some more. Ted blinked, then opened his eyes.

"Where's the rain?"he asked, trying to focus on the ceiling. "How did I get here in the living room? I'm supposed to be up a tree."

After the tension of the morning and our worry over Ted, we all relaxed and laughed.

"You may have been in a tree earlier, sir; but I found you unconscious in the ditch beside the highway,"the agent said.

Ted looked puzzled, as he said, "Tree, road. Now I

remember. I spotted someone crouching in a tree about twenty yards away. I thought it might be one of the kids poaching, so I called out to him. Then something hit me, and that's the last thing I remember."

CHAPTER EIGHTEEN

While Ted was telling us what had happened up on the road, we heard a truck shift into low gear and make its way down our driveway. As we sat tense and listening, two other trucks ground to a stop in front of our place.

"Now what?"Lew said, going to the door. "Oh, hi, folks, come on in and join the party."

I left Ted's side and saw Abe Curtis and Harry Burns climb down from Abe's truck. "Come on, guys,"Abe called to the drivers of the other trucks. "Time for today's orders." As he and Harry mounted the porch steps, he added, "We brought along more men to help in the search. Where do you want us to start this morning?"

"No need, Abe. The kids are back with their parents,"Frank Allen said, walking over and shaking hands with Abe and Harry.

I suppressed a giggle as I watched Frank pad over to the trucks in Ted's robe. His hairy legs did nothing to enhance the view for me.

"Safe? Great! Where did you find them?"Harry asked to Frank's retreating back.

"Not far from here,"Frank answered as he walked over and introduced himself to the other drivers. Coming back with them to our house, he added, "There is something you can do that might give us a lead on this kidnaping."

"What's that?"one of the men asked.

"Check on rental cars you see in town, on out-of-state

licenses parked at motels, recent rented houses."

"In the tourist season? You have to be kidding,"Harry said.

"I don't kid, Mr. Burns,"Frank said. "Can you men do this for us?"

"We'll give it a try,"Abe said. "Who gets our reports?"

"The sheriff or his deputies. Ready to start?"

"Right now." Turning to the other drivers, Abe said, "You, Chuck, take the north side of town; and you, Cal, try the south end. Harry and I'll take a listen around town and check on the new rentals."

When the men gave the OK signal, they and Abe and Harry left us and drove off.

Before the dust of the departing trucks was settled, Frank stuck his head back in the door and said he was going to have another look down at the beach. "And around the tree where Ted spotted the crouching man. I'll be back to talk to the little guys, when they wake up."

While Frank had been giving instructions to Abe and the others, I saw B.C. slip out of the bathroom and tap on the door to the boys' room.

Even with a towel wrapped around her wet head, she looked better than I did in my flowered mumu. Lora answered the knock and beckoned B.C. to come in with her and the sleeping boys.

There had been so many people milling around our living room and porch that I hadn't noticed Eddie leave. I was opening a can of soup when he appeared in the doorway to the kitchen. He carried a package under his arm and a puzzled look on his face.

"Frank around?"he asked.

"No, but he will be back in a little while. What's the matter?"Ted asked, shifting gingerly on the couch. "Come sit down, son. You look as if the world's resting on your shoulders."

Eddie ignored the question and comment. Instead he settled into a chair and asked, "How's the head, Dad?"

"Sore, but I'll live. Now what's bothering you?"

I sidled into the room to listen.

"It's these prints. I took them to a local photo lab and had a couple blown up. Frank has to see them."

Before he could tell us more about the prints, the door to the boys' room opened. Will and Tom were wiping sleep out of their eyes as they came into the room with their parents and B.C.

"Grandma, I'm hungry,"Tom said and put his head in my lap. Kissing his freshly combed hair, I said, "What's it to be, a milkshake, a sandwich?"

Will, nestled at my side, answered for both of them. "Peanut butter sandwiches and milkshakes, Grandma. With lots of chocolate."

While the boys ate, Frank returned. Smiling at the boys, he asked, "Had a good nap?" When they nodded with chocolate milk coating their lips, he said, "Why don't you tell us about your recent adventure?"

They looked at their parents. When Lew said, "Tell them, boys," they put down their sandwiches and began their tale.

"We saw Grandpa and Uncle Eddie on the beach. They looked too busy to talk with us, so we started back to find Dad and Mama,"Will said.

"But then we stopped to play leap frog,"Tom added.

"And you fell over me,"Will said, giving his brother a punch on the arm. "You rolled over on your back in those stickers."

"Yeah, big help you were. Just stared at something caught in the bushes,"Tom said.

"What was it, Will?"Frank asked, leaning forward.

"The tiniest radio I ever saw." Will hesitated, then continued. "That's the last I remember."

"You went to sleep when that guy in the funny outfit covered your face with a rag,"Tom said.

"Funny outfit?" Frank said.

"Yes. A bear suit. When he came over to me, I thought he wanted to give me a bear hug. I don't know what happened next,"Tom said.

"It was dark when I woke up,"Will said. "I couldn't move my hands or feet."

"Were you outside on the ground?"Frank asked.

"Inside some place on a hard floor. Tom was next to me."

Tom interrupted his brother and said, "After a while the bear came in and brought us spaghetti and a glass of milk. I fell asleep before I finished eating."

"Me too,"Will said. "Next thing I remember was when two bears came and picked us up. It was still dark outside."

"They took us to something that sounded like a helicopter,"Tom said. "Next thing I knew the bears were lifting us into the air," Will cut in on his brother. "Then I fell asleep again."

"Didn't you hear that splash, when we landed in the water?"Tom asked.

"No, but I felt cold, salty water wash across my face. I couldn't wipe it off, because my hands were still tied. Something touched my shoulder. Maybe it was one of the bears."

Tom interrupted Will and said, "I heard that helicopter. It got louder, then seemed to be moving away from us."

"Yeah, I heard it too. Real loud at first then I couldn't hear it. I felt I was rocking on water, and I got scared.,"Will said.

"I thought we were going to die,"Tom said and started to cry. I saw Lew gulp to hold back his tears before gathering both of his sons in his arms. Turning to Frank, he said, "That's enough. No more questions."

Frank nodded and thanked the boys. "You've been real F.B.I. men. I may hire you some day."

Tom and Will perked up at Frank's words and said they would help any time.

"I'll give you a call,"Frank said and patted Will's head. "Now, I'd better get back to work,"he added, getting up and starting for the door.

"Wait a minute. I'll go with you,"Eddie said, picking up the parcel with the prints. "I have something to show you." The two went over to Frank's car and drove off.

Ted was yawning, and the children were again dozing. Cradling the youngsters, Lora and Lew went to their bedroom and shut the door.

"Nap time for you, Ted,"I said, going over and kissing him. "Still hurt?"I asked, touching his bandage.

"Plenty, but at least I don't have a black eye like you had the other day."

"Just jealous, aren't you?"

"Sure am,"he replied and threw me a kiss on his way to our bedroom.

When the house was quiet, I pulled out my trampoline and began my exercise for the day. How many days had I missed a workout with all the company and excitement? "Can't let myself get flabby,"I muttered as I bounced up and down and hummed to myself. I hadn't done more than ten minutes of work on it when Abe Curtis drove up.

"Darn,"I said and went out to meet him. There was a woman in the truck with him.

"Alice!"I said when I was close enough to see who it was. "When did you get back?"

"About an hour ago. I sure surprised Abe. Flew into San Francisco and came up here on the bus. When I saw Abe's truck parked in front of Joe's real estate office, I walked over there and climbed in the truck to wait for him."

While we talked, I studied this skinny woman whose face had even more wrinkles than mine. Her stringy, mouse-colored hair hung limply around her ears. She had looked more attractive in the curlers she wore the night of the fire at their place than she did this afternoon.

She caught me staring at her and said, "Do I look that bad?"

I had the grace to blush at her question. "Maybe it was your long trip, Alice. A flight across country is enough to wear out anyone." Opening the truck door, I invited them in for a cold drink.

"Any luck in the hunt for the kidnappers, Abe?"I asked as I brought them each a glass of iced tea.

"Not so far. I've been checking on rentals. There are lots of them this time of year, and Harry and I are checking out every one of them." Glancing around the room, he asked, "Where's Ted, and how are the little boys?"

"The whole family is sleeping, except me." I didn't mention Eddie.

While we sipped our drinks, Alice told me about her vacation. "It was good to visit the folks, but I can't stand the heat in Omaha. I could hardly wait to get back here and breathe the fog again,"she said, sniffing the salt air.

"Well, you missed a couple of good foggy nights. Couldn't see to the end of the yard,"I said. Refilling their glasses, I asked whether they would continue to stay with Harry Burns.

"Probably, until we get a place of our own,"Abe said.

"You mean rebuild or rent a trailer to put on your property?"I asked.

"We haven't decided,"Alice said. "In fact Abe and I have a lot of decisions to make. We might look for a place up on the ridge where those new homes are going in. Fancy places. Great view of the ocean in spots, and I could still breathe that good salt air."

When she stopped to take a sip of her tea, Abe said, "I was telling Alice about an offer I had yesterday on our old place, even with the house gone."

"Did you take an option on a piece of property up on the ridge while you were visiting with Joe at his real estate office?"I asked. "Seems there are a lot of sales around here lately."

"You're right. Lots of land speculation, but Joe says it's because folks are fed up with living in the Bay Area or Los Angeles. When they retire or get a little extra money, they flee from the city problems and come up here,"Abe said.

I don't know what made me blurt it out, but I asked whether they had read about converting moon rocks and sea water to form a new source of energy.

"You've been reading too much science fiction, Kay, "Abe said and laughed.

"No, she hasn't. I did read that in the newspaper recently. Something about a bunch of weird scientists playing games with moon rocks and sea water. Russians and Japanese, weren't they?"Alice asked.

"And Americans,"I added. "I was fascinated by the idea.

Weren't you?"

"Crazy. I guess those birds have to work on something to get the grants for their laboratories,"Alice said.

While she was talking, Tom and Will ran out and climbed in my lap. When they saw that I had company, they grew shy. Tom even sucked his thumb.

"You know Mr. Curtis,"I said. "And this is his wife, Alice - Mrs. Curtis, to you."

Tom stared at Alice and said, "Where are your curlers?"

Alice burst out laughing when I scolded Tom for his rudeness. "Do I look better with curlers, boys?"she asked and quickly added, "Don't answer that. So you were there the night of our fire."

They nodded and said, "Everybody was."

While the children settled down on the floor at my feet, Ted came out to join us.

"Good to see you, Alice. Nice trip?"he asked, shaking her hand.

"OK, but it's not California,"she replied.

Abe winked and said, "She missed me. That's why she hurried back." Glancing at his watch, he added, "I'd better get on with checking on newly rented houses for that F.B.I. man. Real crusty, isn't he?"

"A good description of Frank,"Ted said. "But he's a cracking good investigator." As Alice and Abe got up to leave, Ted said, "Glad you're back, Alice. You two drop in any time."

The Curtises passed Frank's car coming into our lane and waved. Another session with Frank. Would I ever get back to my trampoline?

"Wasn't that Mrs. Curtis in the car with Abe?"Eddie asked, when he and Frank walked into the room.

"Yes, she looks a little peeked from her trip,"I said. Seeing Eddie put the package with the prints on the table, I asked, "Anything important on those prints you had enlarged?"

Eddie didn't answer.

"No sense in trying for secrecy with your mother,"Frank

said. "Better tell her and your dad."

"Thanks, I think,"I muttered to Frank, as I watched Eddie pull the enlarged prints from the package.

Turning to us, Eddie said, "Come take a look."

I squinted at the photos but saw nothing unusual until Eddie pointed to a spot and said, "See that dark place? It's a hole."

I bent over closer and looked at the enlargement. There was a hole, all right, and something else.

Will, who had pushed his way in front of me, was staring at the picture.

"Uncle Eddie, something's in the hole. What is it?"

"Mr. Allen and I weren't sure what it was. I knew where I'd taken that shot, so the two of us went over and checked it out while the folks here entertained the Curtises. We crawled on our bellies up to the spot, hoping no sniper was around to cut us off. Using my flash light, we saw what you are looking at, a state-of-the-art transmitter. A strange place for a transmitter, don't you think?"

No one spoke for a minute as we took turns looking at this powerful sender. Why was it here?

CHAPTER NINETEEN

"Why is it here, and who put it here?" I asked. No one, except Will, had an answer.

"To send messages," Will said, breaking the tension for everyone.

"Sure, young fellow, but who put it here is the big question," Frank said. "And why in this unlikely spot?"

"What better spot for signaling a fishing boat lying off the coast?" Ted said.

"Could be, but why would the Curtises want to contact someone out at sea in this secretive manner?" Eddie asked.

"We don't know whether the Curtises put it here or if they even know it's on their property," Ted added. "I wonder how long it's been hidden here."

"It has to be since the fire," I said. "Remember, we crawled all over Abe's land the night of the fire. We'd have seen this, wouldn't we?"

"Not necessarily," Eddie said. "Although I was taking pictures for you, Frank, I could have been standing on top of this hole and never known its contents."

"And I wasn't about to stick my hand in a hole in case I met a snake," I said.

"Maybe whoever started the fire removed the transmitter before setting the blaze," Ted said.

"The arsonist? Could be, but when did he put it back in the

133

hole?"I asked. "They are still checking on the fire, aren't they, Frank?"

Frank didn't answer, just frowned before turning to Will and Tom. "You told us you boys were playing leap frog the day you were kidnaped. And one of you fell over the other and rolled into some stickers."

"And stared at something, didn't you, Will?" Tom asked.

Will nodded. "The tiniest radio I'd ever seen."

"And then the bear came up behind you and covered your face,"Tom said.

"Leap frog, bear, arsonist, transmitter, kidnapper? What's it all mean?"Ted said.

While we were mulling over this find, Lora and Lew joined us. The boys ran to their parents and began telling them everything. "And we found it,"Tom yelled.

"Hush,"Frank said. "This is a secret among us. No one else is to know anything about the transmitter. Got it, kids? Mum's the word."

"What are you going to do about it, Frank?"I asked.

"Top secret, Kay, " he said, taking the enlargements from Eddie and tramping out the door to his car.

I stomped out to the kitchen to start dinner.

While we ate, Eddie announced he was going to stop spying and get back to his job of photographing for his company. "Can you help me, Lew?"

Before Lew could answer, Ted spoke up. "What about me? I'm the roper around here."

"Sorry, Dad. I thought you would want to take a day or two to get over your bruises."

"Nonsense. I'll be ready first thing in the morning. And you two,"he said, turning to Will and Tom. "Stay here or come down with your folks. Don't go running off on your own."

"No, Grandpa. We're too scared to do that again,"they promised.

When we turned on the news before going to bed, there was Frank Allen telling about the rescue of Will and Tom. "Thanks to all you good folks in town for helping us,"he concluded.

The next morning I drove with Lew to drop off Ted and Eddie at their starting point for photographing. As we passed the Curtis property, I noticed a lot of activity. There was a crew clearing the shrubbery near the burned area and one over by the stream separating the Curtises from the land to the north.

"Abe must be serious about selling,"I said.

"Or else the F.B.I. may be taking another look,"Lew said.

We watched Ted and Eddie climb under the fence and plod through the underbrush to the edge of the cliff. Ted tested the loop in his rope and tossed it over Eddie's head. Eddie tightened it and began his descent. I knew I'd be nervous until they returned to the house for lunch.

"Why did Eddie have to choose this dangerous line of work,"I muttered to Lew.

"He'd be bored with an office job, Mom."

When Eddie's head disappeared over the edge of the cliff, Lew shifted into drive and continued on up the road to the post office. "Need anything at the store?"he asked.

"Maybe a gallon of milk for the boys' milk shakes,"I said.

As we neared the town, Lew said, "Let's eat out tonight. My treat."

"Don't you like my cooking?"

"It's not that. I'm sick of hearing the change of the guard. How much longer are we going to be trapped on your own property?" As he slowed to avoid hitting a group of Boy Scouts hiking along the road, he added, "And folks dropping in at the house any hour of the day. I swear it's quieter in the city than up here."

I leaned over and touched his hand on the steering wheel. "OK. Dinner out tonight. I'm sorry you've had such a dreadful visit. First Lora's miscarriage, then the fire, my brush with death, the kidnaping, the assault on Dad. Oh, yes, the car accident and a couple of deaths and the attack on Joe Gilliam. We usually don't entertain in this fashion."

"Cut the sarcasm, Mom. Don't you realize you are living in

the midst of a terrible mess? Someone may be stalking you at this very minute. We have to get you and Dad out of here."

"No way, son. This is our home. Oh, look,"I said, rolling down the window and pointing. "There's Harry at the filling station."

"Mom, roll up the window. I don't want to talk to anybody, except you, right now."

"Kind of grouchy this morning, aren't you? To humor you I'll duck if Harry spots us, but there's a price you have to pay for my concession."

"What's that?"

"Treat me to pecan rolls at the bakery."

I was happy to see a smile flicker across Lew's face as he agreed to my request.

On the way back to the house we discussed eating places and chose a fish house for tonight. As I was getting out of the car, Lew said, "I'm going over to the county seat again to sniff around about land sales. Want to come?"

"No thanks. Take Lora. She needs a break. The boys and I'll be fine. Maybe I'll drive us over to the park for a picnic."

"Don't get into trouble while I'm gone,"he said, and grinned.

As soon as Lora and Lew left for the county seat, I packed a picnic lunch while the boys got out their fishing tackle. We settled on a knoll overlooking the river to eat our lunch. I dozed while the boys fished. No whistles, no drop-in company, no mysterious phone calls. Lovely! These last two weeks had been awful. I hoped our troubles were over, but I doubted it.

When we returned to the house in the late afternoon, we found Ted and Eddie asleep. We tiptoed out to the car port and put our newly caught and cleaned fish in the freezer.

Before I had time to wash the fish smell off my hands, Tom came out of the bedroom holding his favorite book. He and Will climbed on the couch beside me, and I started to read to them. By the time I finished the story, both of them were sound asleep. I put my head back among the cushions and closed my eyes.

The sound of a car door roused us from sleep. Will rubbed his eyes, then rushed out the door to welcome his parents. Will ran behind him yelling, "Mama, Dad!"

Lew could hardly contain his excitement. He had found that the Curtis property was in escrow. "Also the lots on both sides of Abe's place have recently changed hands, and there's more,"he said, laying out the papers he had brought home with him. "That area on the other side of the road from Abe's - no one's lived there for a long time - was sold day before yesterday."

"What's going on around here?"Ted asked as he came out of our bedroom.

"A lot of property is suddenly changing hands, Dad. What does that mean to you?"

"I don't know. Good business for the real estate folks, I guess."

While we were discussing the property sales, Eddie came out of his room and added his opinion. "I think there's a blitz by some out-of-town outfit to get its hands on land up here and force its rezoning for condominiums. Dreadful thought!"

"Forget dreadful thoughts and hop in the car,"Lew said, gathering his papers and carrying them into the bedroom. "We're going over to the pier for dinner. Who wants to ride in front with me?"

"Me. . . me,"Tom and Will cried at once and wrestled over the seat.

"OK, OK. Both of you can be up here. Tom, sit on your mother's lap. Will, be my pilot and sit here in the middle." Watching us squeeze into the back seat, Lew added, "I hope it's not too crowded for the three of you."

"Just cozy,"I said, tucking my feet on the two sides of the floor divider.

While we ate, we watched several fishing boats heading for the commercial cove a mile or so north of us. Gulls accompanied them, and swooped close to the tantalizing catch on deck. The sky was a glorious red tonight, and the old saying kept repeating itself in my brain, "Red sky at night, sailors' delight."

We talked with neighbors who were also enjoying a meal out. Abe and Alice Curtis were treating Harry Burns to a fish dinner. On their way out, they stopped to chat with us. Harry and Abe had to get to bed early tonight, they said.

"We'll be out fishing before you folks are awake, "Harry said. "We hear the rock cod's biting."

"Good luck," Ted said.

"We might bring you a big one,"Abe said as he and the other two walked toward the exit.

The red sky's promise of a clear day proved true. The glare of the morning sun woke me earlier than usual. Taking a pail with me, I descended to our cove and played in one of the tide pools. Carefully avoiding the clutches of the sea anemone, I searched for a sand dollar to take to the boys. Before going back to the house, I climbed up and sat on one of the rocks to watch the waves roll into shore. There was so much power, yet peace, here where the ocean and the beach met. Only the shouts of the grandchildren calling down to me reminded me it was time to prepare breakfast. Reluctantly I left my favorite retreat and mounted the steps to the top of the cliff.

As soon as Ted and Eddie finished breakfast, they picked up their equipment in preparation for another day of photographing, "What surprises will we find this morning, Dad?"Eddie asked as they started out the door.

"None, I hope,"Ted answered.

They had been gone only a few minutes, when Frank Allen drove into the yard. Slamming his car door, he yelled, "Where are those great neighbors of yours, Curtis and Burns?"

"How should I know?"I said. "What's the matter?"

"The chopper's down and I need Harry's plane. I can't find him anywhere. Did he think one or two days of checking for the kidnappers was enough?"

"Calm down, Frank. They have gone fishing and probably won't be back until sundown,"Lew said, and added, "Can we help?"

"Fishing! Just when I could use their help." Dropping into a chair, Frank said, "Isn't anybody going to offer me a cup of coffee?"

"Boy, you're in a great mood,"I said, zapping a cup in the microwave for him. "Aren't you going to answer Lew? He volunteered to help, if possible."

"Sorry. No sense in biting off your heads." Looking at Lew, he said, "Yes, you can help. I need someone to pick up Joe Gilliam over in Santa Rosa."

"Joe Gilliam? He's strong enough to be back on duty?"I asked.

"Says he is, and we need him."

"I'll drive over and get him, Frank,"Lew said. "Harry's plane would have been faster, but Joe can enjoy the Burbank gardens, while he's waiting for me. Tell him that when you contact him." Getting his car keys, Lew turned to Lora and the boys and asked, "Coming?"

"I'll be right there,"Lora answered as Will and Tom raced to the car.

On the way out the door, Lew asked where he should pick up Gilliam.

"At the gardens since you're sending him there like a regular tourist,"Frank said and added, "Thanks, Lew. Gilliam can sniff the roses or whatever is in bloom while he waits."

"Putting down his cup, Frank grinned at me and said, "I haven't thought of a good snoop job for you yet, Kay."

"With you as my boss, I'm sure it will be a thrill,"I retorted as Frank started down the steps.

At last the house was quiet. I pulled out my trampoline and did twenty minutes of jumping on it before walking to the post office to get the mail and pick up a newspaper. Alice was at the post office sorting her mail, when I stepped in the door.

"Hope you have some good news,"I said to her when I saw her slitting open one of the envelopes.

She had her back to me and turned with a start when I spoke. "Oh, hi, Kay. I didn't see you come in. Good news, you say. Just another bill; and that's not good news, is it?"

I shook my head and asked if she would like to stop at the cafe for a cold drink before going back to Harry's place.

"Sure. I'll wait until you pick up your mail and walk over with you,"she said, opening another envelope.

Over cokes at the restaurant, Alice told me about her sister in Omaha. "A real joiner - women's groups, a garden club, a bridge foursome, the country club. She tried to get me to buy a set of clubs and take lessons from her pro while I was there. I had to come home in self defense,"she added.

"Maybe you can start your own club if you move into a condominium up on the ridge,"I said as we paid for our drinks.

"And that's what we're going to do, move up there. We put a down payment on one of the condos yesterday. It should be ready within sixty days, the contractor said."

"You've sold your property?"I asked.

"Yes, it's in escrow. Abe did it for me." Her eyes filled with tears as she added, "I couldn't move back onto the old lot, no matter how beautiful the new house there might be. The memory and smell of the fire would always be with me."

I hadn't realized how sensitive Alice was. Then, we hadn't been close friends.

On the way back to our house, I thought about Abe and Alice. They had been through a lot this past month. First those threats that Abe reported on TV. Shortly after that, the explosion. "The insurance company must have paid well, if they can move into one of those fancy condominiums,"I muttered with a touch of jealousy.

I hadn't noticed when I left the restaurant; but, by the time I was rounding the last curve in the road leading to our house, a cold wind had sprung up. Dark clouds covered the sun. The sea had turned an angry green. So much for the old saying about sailors' delight with a red sky at sunset.

Suddenly I thought about Abe and Harry. They were probably still out fishing. Surely they had heard the weather report. I hoped they were heading to shore. As I turned into our driveway, the first drops of rain dampened my hair and ran down my nose.

CHAPTER TWENTY

When I walked into the house, I turned on the TV for the noon news. "A small craft warning has been issued by the Weather Bureau,"the announcer was saying. "The spattering of rain we are receiving at the moment is just the edge of a big storm that is moving toward the coast. It should hit our area, full force, early this evening."

A chill went through me. Would Harry and Abe get caught in the storm? Closer to home, I began to worry about Ted and Eddie. They should be back by now, I thought.

While I was stewing about them, I heard Ted's car coughing into our driveway.

"What's the matter with the car?"I asked when they came up the steps.

"We don't know. It sounded fine on our drive to our photo spot this morning; but, when we turned on the engine to come home, we heard this hacking noise."

"You should have stopped at Hal's garage on your way here,"I said. "You two! The car could break down on you, and you'd still be talking about the last swing out over a cliff."

"Of course. That would be much more interesting than checking out a wheezing car,"Ted said and added, "Stop being such a worry wart. I'll take her to Hal's this afternoon."

"She probably needs some minor adjustment, and you know how handy with cars Dad and I are,"Eddie said.

I smiled, remembering the last time they had tinkered with a car. Disaster!

Over lunch Eddie talked about the morning's work. "That should finish my assignment. I'll go in with you, Dad, and get the film developed. Maybe enlarge a couple of shots." Turning to me, he said, "Mom, you should see Dad, a real wrangler, handles the rope like a pro."

Ted glowed with both embarrassment and pride.

While I was admiring my husband for his new found talent, he said, "Won't you stay and have a real vacation with us before you have to report to your home office, Eddie?"

"I was hoping you'd ask. Sure I'll stay a few more days. Besides, I met a former college classmate at the store the other morning. A real looker. I promised her we'd get together to catch up on the news about each other."

"Who is she? Anybody we know?"I asked.

"Jennie Locher. You never met her. She was a mouse of a girl in college; but man, has she changed!"

Ted winked at me. Pushing his chair back from the table, he said, "We'd better get into town and to the garage before all hell breaks loose in this storm."

The rain was now pounding on the roof, and the wind was bending the trees almost to the ground. As I watched Ted and Eddie run for the car, I saw a large pine cone drop on Ted's head and bounce off. I tried not to think of Lew and his family on their drive back from Santa Rosa.

After Ted spun the car in the loose, wet gravel and took off, I settled down with the newspaper and my crossword puzzle. "An eight-letter word for 'ruse'", I muttered. "Ah, 'intrigue.'"

I was finishing the puzzle and beginning to worry about both Ted and Lew and their passengers when Lew and Lora drove into the yard. I held the screen door open for them, as they ran dripping into the house. Not the boys! They raced around outside, splashing mud on themselves and shouting with glee over the rain. A couple of hours cooped up in the car were more than they could stand.

"I'll let them strip on the porch, Mom, and stick them in the shower after they have run off some of their excess steam,"Lora said, and headed for the bedroom to change her soaking clothes.

Now that the little family was safely inside, I began fretting about Ted and Eddie. They should be back from the garage by now. I hadn't long to fret, before they turned into the driveway. However, instead of Ted's usual cheery greeting, he was quiet as he climbed the porch steps. Eddie didn't say anything, just gave me a peck on the cheek and disappeared into his room.

Taking Ted's wet jacket and hanging it in the kitchen, I said, "Get the car fixed?"

Ted nodded as he sat down in the big chair and motioned for me to join him. A frown played across his face.

"What's wrong?"I asked.

He hesitated before speaking. "That little cough you heard from our car was a warning to us. Someone had planted a bomb under the hood. Fortunately, it was a dud."

"Oh, no,"I sobbed and buried my face on his shoulder.

Lew, who had dried off and changed, came into the room, as Ted told me about the bomb. "Dad, what are you talking about? A bomb? Your car?"

While Ted was giving us the full details of taking the car to Hal and finding the bomb, Lora came in and sat down on the floor beside Ted and me. When he finished talking, she cried, "Dad, you and Eddie could have been killed."

Lew took charge. "Let's cut out the histrionics. What kind of bomb was it? Any finger prints? Where were you parked today? Have you told Frank Allen?"

Ted gave a nervous laugh and said, "Not so fast, son. Yes, I phoned Frank immediately." Glancing at me, he added, "Remembered the number, Kay."

We had almost forgotten about the boys in our concern over the bomb until they came bursting into the room carrying a dead rat. So much for stripping off clothes on the porch!

"Can we have a funeral for it?"Will asked.

Lew kept his cool as he said, "Let's give it a sailor's

farewell." Looking out the door, he added, "The rain's abated for the moment. We'll say a few words and toss it over the cliff and watch the tide take it out to sea."

While the three of them were gone, Lora and I cleaned up the muddy mess on the floor. On the boys' return from the ceremony for the rat, they were hustled into the bathroom for showers and a change of clothes. At the insistence of Lora, they settled on their bed for a quiet reading time. And to give us adults a chance to mull over the near accident to Eddie and Ted.

Lew again took charge. "About any prints? What did Frank say?"

Eddie, who had left the room he shared with Will and Tom, replied. "Frank didn't hold much hope for them. Probably smeared beyond use, but he sent one of his agents over to the garage to lift any possible good ones."

"I wish we could get a team of experts up here from the Valley to handle this investigation,"Lew said. "We have one of the best in the world in our area."

"Stop bragging. Frank will do a fine job,"Ted said.

Lew ignored his father and said, "Let's start at the beginning. Where were you parked? "

"On the road beside the Higgins' place. That's where we were doing my last photographing,"Eddie said.

"See anyone stop?"

"How could we? I was dangling in space, and Dad was working the rope."

While we were mulling over this question, the telephone rang. I jumped up to answer it. It was Alice Curtis.

"Have you heard the news?"she sobbed.

"What news"I said.

"About the missing fishing boats. Abe's is one of them."

"I'm so sorry. Do you want us to come stay with you?"

"Can you? I'm so scared,"Alice said.

"Ted and I'll be right over. You are still at Harry's place, aren't you?"I asked.

"Yes. Be careful. The storm's awful."

While I checked for food Lora could fix for dinner, Lew turned on the radio. We listened to the repeated warning to boat owners. Even those that were moored should be lashed against this storm. The one fishing boat that was still missing belonged to Abe Curtis. "Only two people reported aboard that vessel,"the announcer said. "A Coast Guard cutter is still searching in spite of the rough sea. Reconnaissance planes are grounded by the weather."

I grabbed my raincoat and followed Ted to our car, thanking God that the bomb was no longer in it. Alice was waiting for us at the door of Harry's place.

"Thanks for coming,"she said. Taking our wet coats, she asked, "Did you listen to the radio? His is the only boat that hasn't come in! How much longer can the Coast Guard keep looking today?"she cried.

"A few more hours, perhaps,"Ted said, walking over to the fireplace and throwing on another log. "You know both Abe and Harry are good seamen. They are probably moored a few miles up the coast waiting out the storm."

"Then why hasn't Abe contacted me?"

"I don't know,"Ted said.

The three of us lapsed into silence as we listened to the wind shriek around us and the rain beat against the windowpanes.

Somewhere in the house a short wave radio crackled to life. Alice rushed from the room.

"Maybe that's Abe,"I said.

Before Ted could respond, Alice slipped back into the room.

"Was it Abe?"Ted and I both asked at once.

Alice frowned and said, "No. Just a friend of Harry's wanting to talk with him."

As I reached and turned on a table lamp, 1 saw a bolt of lightning cut across the dark sky. Almost immediately we heard a clap of thunder, followed by a tremendous crash outside. The lights went out. Terrified, we walked to the floor- to- ceiling window and saw sparks spitting from a transformer across the road. A huge pine tree lay across the power line.

"Where does Harry keep his kerosene lantern?"I asked.

"And how about candles and matches?"Ted added.

Alice stumbled back from the window and said, "I don't know. Maybe the matches and candles are in that high cupboard in the kitchen. The lantern? Try the garage, Ted."

"Without a flash -light? Wait. I have one in our car. I'll go get it,"he said, and dashed out in the storm.

I was already pushing a chair toward the cupboard as Alice spoke and was feeling along the shelves when Ted returned with the flash- light. Alice didn't seem able to move and help. What was the matter with her? Probably overcome with worry about Abe.

With the help of the flash -light Ted found a kerosene lantern in the garage. Fortunately the can of kerosene oil was next to it on the garage floor. Within a few minutes he had poured in the oil, adjusted the wick and lighted the room.

Now I saw the candles and their holders tucked in the back of the top shelf of the cupboard. I handed them to Alice who busied herself carrying the candles to various parts of the house to light when needed. She brought a warm glow to the living room with three of the taller candles.

"Here, give me one of the candles, Alice. I have to notify the sheriff about that tree across the power line,"Ted said.

Alice shook her head and said she would call the sheriff on the short wave. Taking one of the candles, she disappeared into the room where we had earlier heard the short wave squawk to life.

Having no more desire to look out into the now black night, I closed all the drapes. The lantern and candles cast dancing lights on the living room walls and gave me a sense of coziness, although nothing could drown out the scream of the wind.

With the road blocked, it looked as if we would have to spend the night here. We needed to let our family know. I reached for the telephone. The line was dead. "Now, how do we reach Lew and Eddie?"

"Easy. I'll get them on the short wave,"Alice said, coming back into the living room. "You do have a set, don't you?"

"Yes, and I keep it open at all times as the sheriff has warned all of us living up here to do. Thanks, Alice."

"And don't forget to tell them about the tree over the road,"Ted called to Alice's retreating back.

"I'm hungry,"Ted said when we were alone. "I saw a Coleman stove out in the garage when I was rummaging for the lantern. I'll get it and pump in some fuel. Look for something to eat, Kay."

"Hey, this isn't our house. We'll ransack the place when Alice returns,"I said.

"Did I hear my name?"Alice said as she and her flickering candle came into view.

"Yes. I have a starving husband who is demanding his dinner. What do you have to offer the three of us?"I asked.

"Thanks to the Coleman stove Ted is holding, we can have hamburgers with potato chips. I think there are enough salad ingredients. Take a look in the refrigerator, Kay."

We lingered over our after dinner coffee and reminisced about our lives before coming to the Mendocino coast. By ten o'clock, we were bored with our own conversations and ready for bed. Alice found a pair of pajamas for Ted and loaned me one of her sexy nightgowns. Sexy? I hadn't thought of Alice as sexy; but, then, there was a lot I didn't know about my neighbor.

Huddled in the blankets Alice gave us, we settled down on the couch by the fire. I must have fallen asleep almost immediately. The next thing I knew, I was chilled. Ted was snoring beside me. I slipped off the couch and added another log to the dying fire, bringing it back to life. The wind had died down, and the steady quieter rain put me back to sleep.

The squawk of the short wave radio wakened me some time around dawn. I heard Alice run down the hall to answer it. Now, fully awake, I sat up and waited for her to come out and report any news to us. Nothing. The house was too still. What had Alice learned?

CHAPTER TWENTY-ONE

Now that there was no longer any glow from the fireplace, the room felt dank and gloomy. To cheer me up, I pulled back the drapes and looked out on a bright sky. The storm had passed, and only the scattered pine cones littering the yard reminded me of the wild night we had lived through.

The sunshine pouring in through the east window disturbed Ted who awoke from his sleep and grunted a greeting. "Was that your signal for me to get up?"

"No, but I was lonesome for your company." When he sat up and felt on the floor for his absent slippers, I said, "If you'll pad out to the kitchen and light the Coleman stove, I'll make coffee for the three of us."

"No need to do that, Kay," Alice said, coming into the room. The power is back on, and we can have a real breakfast."

When we sat down to eat, we turned on the radio to catch the morning news. Too late! The announcer was saying, "And that's the update on the damage from last night's storm. More news at noon."Nothing about Abe or Harry.

We were clearing away the breakfast dishes, when we heard a car brake in front of Harry's house. I looked out and saw Lew splashing his way through the puddles toward us. "Road's cleared,"he said as he stopped on the porch to remove his boots before coming in the room.

"Any news about Abe?"Alice asked.

"Yes. The Coast Guard found Abe's fishing boat this morning."

"Where?"Alice asked. "Was Abe in it?"

"God, I hope not. The boat foundered on rocks off the coast north of here, and pieces of it washed ashore."

At these words, Alice screamed and ran from the room.

"You could have broken the news more gently,"I muttered to Lew.

A chagrined Lew turned to us and said, "Maybe Abe and Harry were rescued by a ship that hasn't reported on finding them."

"Rescued in this storm?"I said. "Be real, Lew."

Hearing Alice sobbing in the next room, I opened the door and went to her. "Why don't you come home with us, Alice? We can listen to the news from our place."

"Could I? I can't stand to be alone here,"she said, wiping her damp cheeks with a tissue.

After Alice locked up Harry's house, we made our way to Lew's and our cars and drove toward home. The repair crews were mighty busy today. They had managed to get the tree off the transformer and haul it to the side of the road. This would be fire wood for someone for many months.

"Telephone lines are still down everywhere in town,"Lew said as we dodged another tree partially covering the road near our place.

The day dragged on as we waited to learn more about Abe and Harry's fate. I must have drifted off to sleep. When I awakened, Alice was gone. Ted had left me a note saying he was driving into town with Eddie to mail the last of the photos to his company. Lew, Lora and the boys had gone to the pier to see the wreckage left by the storm.

I looked all around the house and walked up the road calling to Alice. No response. In her distraught condition, she might do something desperate. Perhaps she had gone down to our cove hoping to find Abe still alive but unable to call for help.

I descended the slippery steps to our beach. The tide had

washed debris up against the rocks under the cliff. I knelt down and began collecting driftwood wedged there. My hand touched an oilskin pouch. Maybe Abe and Harry had made it to the shore at this spot and dropped the pouch. There was no other sign that someone had been here since yesterday's storm. Tucking the pouch into my jacket pocket and leaving the driftwood at the bottom of the steps, I climbed to the high ground behind our house. The boys could bring the driftwood up to our wood pile later today or tomorrow.

I went back inside hoping Alice had returned. No one was there. In her present frame of mind, she might have gone to look at the burned out shell of her old home. Or she might have decided to walk the three miles to Harry's. Before I looked any further for Alice, I called the sheriff's office to learn whether there was more news about Abe and Harry. Nothing.

Putting down the phone, I decided to walk over to the Curtises. The road was almost dry after last night's storm. I easily skirted around the few puddles still holding their muddy contents. I heard frogs chirping in the ditch as I jumped across and made my way over the rough ground. Why hadn't I had sense enough to use Abe's driveway, I wondered, when I skinned my knee in falling in one of the shallow holes pocketing the place.

I stopped at intervals and called Alice's name. No answer. When I approached the shell of their former home, I saw no one. Not even a squirrel came down from a charred tree to greet me. Realizing that Alice was not here, I walked back to our place to see whether she or anyone else had returned. The house was empty.

After taking a few minutes to rest and drink a glass of water, I started along the road toward Harry's place. En route, I had to pass the Allison house. Memories of that awful experience there made me shudder. Standing at the foot of the driveway, I recalled Frank Allen and the widow, Mrs. O'Brien, in deep conversation in the yard the morning our family trudged up there, armed with buckets and mops.

While I wool gathered in the driveway, I heard voices coming from the house. It was supposed to be empty, and the "No trespassing"sign didn't encourage visitors. Maybe there were some of Frank Allen's crew in there cleaning up the pizza mess left by Joe and his partner. While I gawked at the house, I heard angry voices shouting at one another. Who was in the house?

Curiosity got the better of me. I tiptoed to the side window hoping to catch a glimpse of Frank scrubbing the floor. Before I could focus my eyes on the room, someone grabbed me and dragged me into the house. I clawed at him trying to get loose from his grip, but it was no use. He was a man I had never seen before. He growled at me in a language I didn't recognize. When I yelled at him to let me go, another person threw a blanket over my head and knocked me to the floor.

I heard that guttural voice saying something. Then another man spoke, "Damn nuisance!"he said, and I felt a sharp kick in my ribs.

"Put her in the closet,"someone hissed close to my ear. There was a familiar odor growing stronger. Just before I lost consciousness, I knew what it was - chloroform!

I don't know how long it was before I awakened. The blanket had been removed, but there was a blindfold over my eyes. I felt my bruised ribs where the man had kicked me. Then I checked my face for any further bruises. When I tried to touch my dry lips, I found my mouth was taped shut. Where was I? Now I remembered. They were going to shove me in a closet. I lay in a fetal position and had trouble straightening my legs. I worked the bandage loose from my eyes, but I still couldn't see. I felt around me, and touched a box, then a broom. There wasn't room for me to stand. I groped for a door; but, when my fingers closed on the latch, I found I was locked in.

CHAPTER TWENTY-TWO

I leaned my head against the door and listened. I caught the sound of low voices in the next room.

"How in the hell did you lose it?"a man snarled.

Now a woman was speaking in that same strange language of the man who had dragged me into the house.

I froze when I heard the next speaker. It couldn't be, I reasoned, but it was Abe Curtis. "I fell and turned my ankle getting out of the raft. Think I could worry about losing it when I wanted to nurse my ankle?"

Then I heard the sharp sound of a slap and a gasp from Abe. "Ouch! Why did you do that? I couldn't help it if I lost the damn thing."

"Fool!"the woman said in English. Was that Alice's voice? It had a guttural sound; yet I was sure it was Alice speaking.

I must have touched the broom, because it scraped across the door and fell to the side of the closet. The voices ceased, and the door opened. Before I could focus on the people in the room, someone shoved a rag with chloroform over my face.

When I next woke up, my stomach ached from hunger; and my head was pounding. I began mouthing nursery rhymes to clear my head. I had to plan my escape if I ever got a chance. Again I leaned against the door and listened. There was no sound, except the scurry of a rat or a squirrel on the roof.

Then I heard it. A door squeaked open, and someone walked toward the closet. Eyes closed, I lay still and pretended to be unconscious. When the door opened, the wreak of garlic from the intruder made me want to vomit.

Muttering in that strange language I'd heard earlier, he covered my face with a chloroform rag, and I blacked out again.

Some time later I woke up. This time my head ached so badly that I almost wished I were dead. No, I had to fight to get out of here. I listened for any talk or approaching footsteps. Silence. I put my head down to the crack under the closet door to try to catch some fresh air. Fortunately, the house wasn't well constructed, and cold air filled my nostrils.

Gaining strength from the fresher air, I again began plotting my escape. I felt around me, and my hand closed over something metallic. It had a wooden handle. Running my hand along its side, I realized this was a screw driver which must have fallen to the floor when the broom slipped.

I inched the screw driver up to the door handle and began to work on the lock. I was lucky; for this was a poorly installed lock, which made it easy to dismantle. Thank goodness, I'd taken that course on how parents survive with children who lock us out of the house! While I tinkered with the door lock, I stopped at intervals to listen for any sound of my captors. I heard nothing.

After what seemed forever, I heard a welcome sound. The lock on the knob on the room side clicked. Reaching for the knob beside me, I opened the door. I was free. I looked all around and listened for any footsteps running down the hall toward the closet. Hearing nothing, I stepped out into the room and peeked out the window.

There was no car in the driveway nor in the carport beside the house. I stepped out onto the porch and waited for any sound from my captors lurking outside. I could easily have been picked off by a sniper as I walked down the driveway and out to the highway. I stayed as close as possible to the ditch by the road and ducked down whenever I saw car lights approaching from either direction. Finally, I spotted our lane. Resting against a post at its entrance, I saw our yard was filled with sheriff's cars. I made my way around them and staggered up the steps and crawled to the door. With my last burst of energy, I stood up and banged on it and almost fell into Ted's arms when he opened the door.

Lights were blazing throughout the house and the living room was filled with people. When I could focus clearly, I saw Frank Allen race to the telephone. Through my mental fog, I heard him bark a message, "She just walked in."

While the family was surrounding me and asking questions, I glanced over Ted's shoulder and looked into a pair of venomous eyes - Alice's! She was standing in the hall entrance and gaping at me. Joe Gilliam was lounging over near the kitchen while a man I'd never seen before was moving toward Alice. I had to warn Frank.

I saw the stranger take Alice by the arm and say,"You shouldn't have to stand there, ma'am. You've had a terrible shock. Come sit over here by the TV."

She simpered a thank you to him. When she was seated, she turned to me and said, "Where have you been? I looked all over for you, when I returned from my walk."

Maybe I was wrong, and that hadn't been Alice's voice I'd heard at the Allison house. While Ted carried me to the couch where the family had made a place for me, I tried to put my suspicions about Alice aside and answer her. "I went looking for you. Where did you go?"

"Just wandered around here and there outside. I didn't want to be far from the phone in case Abe called,"she said. Seeming to notice my dusty appearance, she asked, "Did you fall on your walk?"

"You might say so,"I replied, not wanting to reveal what had happened to me, until I could talk with Frank Allen or to B.C., who was hovering near me.

Lora interrupted and said, "Let her through to the bathroom, so she can clean up. Where have you been, Mom?"she said, taking me away from Ted and leading me out into the hall.

I put my head on her shoulder and whispered, "Get Frank and B.C. for me."

Without breaking step, Lora said, "I bet you're hungry. I'll heat supper while you wash up." With these words she left me at the bathroom door and started toward the kitchen.

I hoped she had my message, but nothing in her manner showed she had understood me. I heard Ted say, "Do you suppose she fell in the ditch? She's usually such a careful walker."

"No, we would have seen her, Dad, when we were searching,"I heard Lew say. "Wait until she gets cleaned up and some supper in her. Then we'll ask her what happened."

When I came out of the bathroom, Frank and B.C. were waiting in the hall. "OK. So you were dumb enough to go down to the beach at dusk. And why roll in the sand, or did you fall off the steps?"Frank said in his usual strident voice. Coming closer to me, he muttered, "Keep up the charade."

Relief swept over me. Lora had understood.

"You could show a little sympathy for a frail woman, Frank."

"I'm really touched by your fragile condition. Did you find any whole sand dollars down there before you stumbled?"

"At this time of year? I have one from last February. It's in the kitchen. Want to see it?"

"OK, I'll look at it; but it better be a whole one. If it is, I'll buy it,"he said, gently nudging me toward the kitchen.

"Step aside, Frank, so I can open the drawer and show it to you,"I said, pulling open a kitchen drawer where I kept this whole sand dollar.

Frank nodded and said, "A beauty. I'll buy it,"he added reaching into his pocket . Instead of money, he slipped a revolver into my hand. Leaning over, supposedly to pick up the sand dollar, he whispered, "It's loaded."

There was a low whistle outside, and the door burst open. "Freeze!"a man said. Behind him were at least a dozen others. Faces peered in at us through the windows. The back door flew open admitting a contingent of Frank's crew, many of whom I'd seen on duty around our place. One of them grabbed Alice as she tried to slip out the back door.

"Let me go," Alice yelled. "Just when I'm in grief, you let your monkeys paw me," she said to Frank.

"Some grief! Your husband is resting comfortably in jail right now along with those two creeps who toady to you," Frank said, and added, "Abe spilled it all, except what you had done with Kay."

"What's going on, Frank?" Ted asked.

"A breakup of an international spy ring, I hope, if the courts have sense enough to convict the members. Let me introduce this agent, your so-called grieving widow, Alice Curtis, better known to INTERPOL as Nazik."

CHAPTER TWENTY-THREE

We stared at Frank, as he continued to talk. "You may have thought the Yakusa, the underworld criminals of Japan, were a bad lot. They are kindergartners in crime compared to this Middle Eastern group. These Middle Easterners have been trying to corner the world market on a new source of energy created by combining helium 3 from moon rocks with hydrogen."

"You mean that stuff Ted and I read about in the newspaper is for real? Helium 3 extracted from moon rocks and hydrogen from sea water?"I asked.

"That's it. It's still on the drawing board. American, Russian and Japanese scientists are debating the possibilities and the ways of getting the moon rocks to earth and where to tap into the best source for the hydrogen. The one chosen for the hydrogen is sea water,"Frank said.

"But how are the Middle Easterners involved?"Ted asked.

"They managed to infiltrate the science labs in the three negotiating countries and found the working plans,"Frank said

"You mean they were going to send up their own space vehicle to bring the rocks to earth? Ridiculous!"Lew said.

"No. Their first project was to locate an isolated stretch of land abutting a large body of sea water. It could be anywhere on the globe. No agency paid much attention to this group of entrepreneurs who were negotiating for a large piece of shore line until three unexplained but similar murders occurred. All three victims were surveyors, marine specialists and known criminals. One was found on the shore of the Aral Sea; another man was found off the coast of Scotland in the North Sea; while the body of the third man came to rest on the shore of the Great Salt Lake in Utah. They each bore a tattoo in Arabic saying, "Glory to Allah." The Utah incident set in motion a call to INTERPOL, a worldwide clearinghouse for police information. According to INTERPOL's records this group planned to seek out a large stretch of beach on the Mendocino Coast."

"That's us,"I cried.

"Yes. With their reactor in place for extracting the sea's hydrogen, they planned to bargain for the right to extract Helium 3 from moon rocks, when the three countries finally signed their agreement to undertake this project."

"Wow! They could then control what the newspapers called the best source of energy for the next several hundred years,"I said. Turning to Ted, I added, "Remember, we read that weird story a few weeks ago."

"Yeah, I remember; but what's Alice have to do with all this?"Ted said.

"Plenty. She's in charge of buying up property here on the Mendocino Coast. She got the ball rolling by ordering the fire on Abe's property." Glancing over at Alice, Frank continued. "Clever piece of work, Nazik. Did you or your lackeys set off the dynamite?"

Nazik, or Alice, as I knew her, spit in the face of the F.B.I. agent holding her.

"How did you get on to her?"Eddie asked.

"INTERPOL has been following her ever since she slipped into the United States a few years ago. Her face was familiar to them as one of the popular Arab entertainers and a spy." Glancing at Will and Tom, Frank said, "That first bear you saw wasn't a man. It was Mrs. Curtis in one of her many costumes. She has danced as Salome, acted the role of Cleopatra and been the dancing bear in a circus."

"Why did she kidnap my sons?"Lora asked.

"She and Abe caught them playing leap frog on the property and peeking into the hole where their transmitter was located,"Frank said.

"Abe? How did he get involved with this woman?"Lew asked.

"He met her on one of his flights in Europe. Remember, he'd been a front man traveling world wide for a chemical company. A lonely widower, he was a perfect dupe for Nazik. She played on his loneliness. She sure didn't look dowdy the way she does today. She was a looker. When he told her about his land out in California on the Mendocino Coast, she set out to marry him. Within a few months, they were married. She got him to take an early retirement for his company and move to the west coast."

"When did he discover who she was and what she planned to do?"I asked.

"INTERPOL didn't get all those details, only that he was soon playing into her hands and doing her bidding,"Frank said.

"Why?"I asked.

"Sex, maybe, but mostly greed,"Frank said and added, "He was no match for this strong woman."

Alice smirked at these words.

Before we could ask other questions, Frank turned to Lew and said, "Thanks for looking up land transactions over at the county seat. That filled in a missing part of our case. Who was buying up the land?" Shifting on the couch, he said, "Those so-called buyers were part of the syndicate.

Since the lands are still in escrow, we can cancel the sales."

When I started to ask another question, Frank stopped me and turned to Eddie, "Your photographs of the area were a real help. Without them we would never have spotted that transmitter in the hole the boys stumbled onto."

Eddie beamed. "Just doing my job,"he said.

"Is Harry Burns part of the gang?"I asked.

"We don't think so, and now we'll never know. His body washed ashore this afternoon,"Frank said. "We started a special search for it, Nazik, when we intercepted your message from Abe over at Harry's house today." Shaking his head, he added, "We couldn't figure out Abe's last words, 'At A this afternoon.'"

"I can tell you that,"I said. "They were meeting at the Allison house." Glaring at Alice - Nazik - I said, "Were you planning to leave me in that locked closet to die?"

"Why not? You're a nuisance,"she answered.

"Mom, you didn't go to the Allison house again, did you?"Lew asked.

"Yes, and I got thrown in a closet and chloroformed. To think that I took the trouble to search down at the beach for you, Alice, or whatever your name is." Reaching into my jacket pocket, I pulled out the oilskin pouch and handed it to Frank. "Is this what Abe dropped when he climbed out of the raft?"

"Oh, my God! Alice gasped, staring at the pouch.

Frank opened the pouch and took out a piece of paper. His face was grim when he finished reading its contents. "The complete plans for the takeover! This should put you away for years, Nazik." Turning to Joe Gilliam, he said, "Take her away and put her under extra guard. She's a slippery one."

"Ouch, you're hurting me,"Alice cried, as Joe grabbed her arm and led her away.

"Not nearly as much as I'd like to for putting out a contract on my partner and me,"Joe growled, but he loosened his grip on her arm. B.C. and another agent stepped to the other side of Alice to make sure she didn't escape.

Had Abe fired the shots that killed Chipped Tooth and Whiny? I wondered. We might never know. The gun could be miles out to sea by this time.

We waited until the car carrying Nazik left and B.C. had run back in the house. Dropping down on the floor beside me, she said, "Well, what's your story, Kay?"

"I recognized Abe's voice, but I wasn't sure about Alice, until I faced her here in the living room. Her shock at seeing me gave her away." I stopped speaking as the memory of that awful time in the closet overwhelmed me. Abe's whining, then the slap.

160

That snarling woman's voice talking in a foreign tongue. The sickening smell of chloroform. Terror at being left locked in the closet. Pushing these thoughts away, I said, "Did Alice put that bomb in Ted's car?"

"No. One of her henchman did that. Confessed about an hour ago,"Frank said. A puzzled look crossed his face, as he asked, "Where did you learn to play Houdini in a locked room?"

"Oh, I got lots of practice as a child. Mother used to lock me in the bedroom when I sassed her, which was often."

"I can believe it,"Frank said.

"And sometimes I had to resort to picking locks when our Lew or Eddie locked me out of the house."

"Mom, I never did that, did I?"Lew asked. "It must have been Eddie."

Watching Eddie punch his brother's arm, I said, "Enough about my adventure. When do I get to eat?"

"How about soup right now while you wait for Lew to throw a steak on the grill?"Lora said and rushed to the kitchen. Lew whipped a steak out of the refrigerator and slapped it on the grill.

"And don't forget the fries,"I called to Lora. "Be sure to make enough fries for my always hungry friend, B.C.,"I added and winked at her.

While the steak sizzled on the grill, I nestled in Ted's arms and listened to Frank take the sting out of the Mendocino menace.

ReGeJe Press Titles

MAID IN THE SHADE Jacqueline Turner Banks 0-9639147-3-1   *Adult Mystery* $13.00

"College-educated cleaning woman, Ruby Gordon, a woman of substance who also has a distinctive, appealing voice is proud of her independence.. Possessed of a quirky good humor delightfully expressed, Ruby herself is the main attraction."   **PUBLISHERS WEEKLY**

POLKADOTS   Geri Spencer Hunter 0-9639147-5-8   *Romance* $13.00

A wickedly seductive mainstream romance that explores the unconventional attraction between a middle-aged black woman and a younger white man.

"Smoothly written, Polkadots is one of those memorable stories that are so easy to pick up and so difficult to put down."
                                                    THE MIDWEST BOOK REVIEW

MURDER BY PROPHECY Maggie Oliver Anderson 0-9639147-4-X *Adult thriller,* $13.00

Allison MacWilliams is running out of time. People are dying all around her and now it looks like they're dying *instead* of her. Could an ancient myth really be the key?

THE SECRET OF ST. GABRIEL'S TOWER Patricia E. Canterbury 0-9639147-6-6 *Juvenile Mystery* $5.99

Ruthie Joan has polio and a house full of brothers and a sister to keep her company until a stranger comes and takes her away. It's the triplets to the rescue.

VALLEY OF THE SHADOW Earl Hardy and Naoma Hardy -0-9639147-8-2 *Adult Horror* $13.99

Tolkien meets Stephen King when four men, each with his own disparate story, confront Pure Evil in a war they won't all survive

"Here we have a pretty good small press horror novel, set in the Old West.. . A good feel for the setting, reasonably good characterization, and some nicely grotesque scenes. . . ."
                                                    SCIENCE FICTION CHRONICLE

MENDOCINO MENACE Beth Howes 0-9639147-0-7 *Adult Mystery* $13.99

Move over Jessica Fletcher, Kay Roberts is on the case. Kay 's peaceful little corner is getting crowded with strange visitors, grandchildren --and bodies